FROM THE
NANCY DREW FILES

THE CASE: A missing baby dolphin leads Nancy into a million dollars' worth of danger!

CONTACT: Arman du Roque, the Rocky Isle Marine Institute's major financial supporter, is running out of money . . . and running out of hope.

SUSPECTS: Matt Folton—Is the television star so committed to animal rights that he's willing to commit crimes that could cost innocent lives?

Dennis Markwood—The institute's head tour guide has come down in the world since his last job. Would a million dollars cushion his fall?

Wendy Zeller—Her romance with the institute's director went sour. Is she seeking some sweet revenge?

COMPLICATIONS: While Nancy looks for the lost baby dolphin, Ned's beginning to wonder what he stands to lose . . . especially with good-looking guide Jason Kalb promising Nancy a personal tour of the institute.

Books in The Nancy Drew Files® Series

Available from ARCHWAY Paperbacks

THE
NANCY DREW FILES™

121

NATURAL
ENEMIES

CAROLYN KEENE

AN ARCHWAY PAPERBACK
Published by POCKET BOOKS
New York   London   Toronto   Sydney   Tokyo   Singapore

This book is a work of fiction. Names, characters, places and incidents are products of the author's imagination or are used fictitiously. Any resemblance to actual events or locales or persons, living or dead, is entirely coincidental.

AN ARCHWAY PAPERBACK *Original*

An Archway Paperback published by
POCKET BOOKS, a division of Simon & Schuster Inc.
1230 Avenue of the Americas, New York, NY 10020

ISBN: 0-671-56879-5

First Archway Paperback printing June 1997

10 9 8 7 6 5 4 3 2 1

Cover art by Bill Schmidt

Printed in the U.S.A.

IL 6+

NATURAL
ENEMIES

Chapter

One

"WHAT DOES BESS *have* in that thing?" Ned Nickerson whispered to his girlfriend, Nancy Drew. He motioned at the gigantic duffel that Bess Marvin was dragging toward them. George Fayne was walking ahead of her with a much smaller bag casually draped over her shoulder.

"I tried to tell her we weren't going to need much," George said when the cousins had reached Nancy's car. "Just jeans, T-shirts, and something dressy for the awards dinner."

Bess dropped her duffel and sat down on it, brushing her long blond hair off her face.

"But she wouldn't listen," George continued as she flung her bag into the trunk of the blue Mustang.

"I didn't want to leave anything behind that

I might need," Bess explained. "And I *know* even now that I forgot something."

Nancy smiled. "Don't worry," she said, holding her hand out to Bess to pull her up. "If you did, you can borrow something of mine."

"Thanks, Nan," Bess said. "You're the best."

"I don't want to break up any female bonding or anything"—Ned picked up Bess's bag with a grunt and dropped it into the trunk—"but let's hit the road, okay? It's going to take us two solid days of driving."

The four friends were on their way to the coastal town of Rockport, Maine, where Ned was to spend his spring break at the Rocky Isle Marine Institute. Ned, who was attending Emerson College, had entered an essay contest about improving the institute. He had won and was awarded a one-week all-expense-paid working vacation there.

When Ned had asked Nancy to join him in preparing the institute's grounds for the upcoming tourist season, she jumped at the chance. Not only would it give her time with Ned, but she'd be supporting a worthwhile cause as well. When she mentioned her plans to George and Bess, they decided to volunteer their time, too.

"Okay." George slammed the trunk closed. "We're ready to go."

"Not quite." Nancy had turned to see Hannah Gruen standing on the porch, a picnic hamper in her hands. "I packed a lunch for you for your first day on the road," Hannah said with a smile. "And some snacks."

"Thanks, Hannah," Nancy said as Ned ran to take the hamper. Hannah Gruen had been with Nancy and her father, Carson Drew, since Nancy was three.

"Yes, thanks, Hannah," Bess added. "Road trips always make me hungry."

George ran a hand through her short, dark, curly hair and shared a grin with Nancy. *"Everything* makes her hungry."

Bess tucked her long blond hair behind her ears and shrugged. "Go ahead and laugh. But I bet Hannah appreciates the fact that I like her cooking."

Hannah joined the girls and said, "I certainly do, Bess. Now, drive safely, and have a wonderful time at Rocky Isle."

"We will," Nancy called as the group piled into her blue Mustang. "See you when we get back in eleven days!"

"If I have to ride in this backseat for one more minute, I'm going to be permanently bent at the waist," Bess groaned.

"Relax, Bess," Ned said from the passenger

seat. He pointed to the map he was reading. "We're in Maine and almost there."

"And if I have to listen to your grumbling one more minute," George warned Bess, "I won't be held responsible for my actions."

Nancy looked through the rearview mirror and laughed. "Come on, you guys. Before we know it we'll be tramping along the rocky coast, breathing fresh salt air."

An hour later, with the sun hanging low in a cloudy late afternoon sky, Nancy pulled the car up to the Rocky Isle Marine Institute.

The buildings that housed the institute had been constructed on the grounds of the family estate of its founder, Arman du Roque. The du Roques had made their fortune in the lumber industry, but Arman du Roque had abandoned the family business to pursue the study and preservation of marine life. Paths cleared through the wooded estate led to seaside cliffs and then down to the ocean. It was those paths, as well as others on several nearby islands, that Nancy, Bess, and George were to help clear for the season opening.

"How beautiful," Nancy said as she stepped out from behind the driver's seat and stretched her arms over her head. Her friends followed.

"I love New England," George said, breathing deeply. "The sea air is so invigorating!"

"And Mr. du Roque's mansion—at least

what I can see of it through the trees—seems pretty spectacular." Ned pointed toward the Gothic-style towers in the distance. "Imagine the view of the ocean from those tower rooms."

Nancy put her arms around Ned's waist. "I think this is going to be a wonderful week," she said, smiling.

"I certainly hope so," said a man from a short distance away. Nancy backed away from Ned to look at the handsome young man approaching them. He was dressed in jeans, work boots, a sweater, and a canvas work jacket.

"And I hope you like backbreaking labor," he added as he came near. "Hi, I'm Jason Kalb, assistant trainer. And you must be Ned Nickerson from Emerson College." Jason put out his hand to shake Ned's.

"Yes, I am," Ned responded. "And this is Nancy Drew, and George Fayne, and Bess Marvin. They're members of your preseason volunteer crew."

"I'm happy to meet you, Jason," Nancy said as she, in turn, shook Jason's hand.

George waved, and Bess, who until that moment had been at the back of the group, emerged and gave Jason a dazzling smile. "Hello, Jason. I'm Bess."

Nancy bit back a grin. When a good-looking

guy was around, Bess could be counted on to flirt.

Jason gave Bess a big smile in return. Nancy saw his ice blue eyes twinkle. "My pleasure," he said. Then he cleared his throat and turned back to Ned and Nancy. "Well, let's get you guys settled. Unfortunately, you'll have to leave your car here at the institute and walk to your housing."

Ned and Jason began to unload the car. "Where are we staying?" Nancy asked.

Jason heaved Bess's bag out of the trunk and instantly dropped it. "Whoa, what's in this thing?" he asked. "Never mind," he added. "I don't think I want to know. Nancy, you, George, and Bess will be sharing a crew cabin behind the institute. The other volunteers, as well as a few of the regular employees, are staying in the other cabins."

"Sounds romantic," Bess said brightly.

"Sounds like roughing it," George amended. "Which is just fine with me."

Jason laughed. "And Ned will be staying at the du Roque mansion." Jason nodded toward the Gothic towers, more difficult to see now as the sky grew darker.

Nancy thrust her arms through her backpack and slung her travel bag over a shoulder. "Okay, let's go get settled."

"This way," Jason said. He indicated Bess's

bag. "Just one thing. Would the owner of this beast mind if I dragged it? I don't think my back can take it."

Bess laughed. "Oh, all right. *I'll* carry it. After all, I did manage to get it to Nancy's house all by myself, didn't I?"

Jason led the way around the administration and lab building and onto a dirt path that looked as if it had been recently cleared.

They hadn't gone far when Jason stopped in front of a charming wood cabin, one of six that were spread out along the path. "Here you are," Jason said. "Home sweet home."

"So when do we start work?" Nancy asked.

"Well," Jason answered, "first you have to get through the awards dinner tonight. It's being held in the museum. Be prepared for a lot of boring speeches and rubber chicken."

Ned smiled. "We'll live. When does the real work begin?"

"Tomorrow morning at seven," Jason answered. "We have a lot to do before the institute opens to the public in two weeks."

"Could you elaborate?" Bess asked. "Like what kind of work, exactly?"

Jason's eyes glittered with mock-evil intent. "Well, winters are tough up here in Maine. No matter how well groomed the grounds are when the institute closes for the winter, by early spring the trails are a total mess. It's up to the volunteers to clear the paths and make them safe for tourists. You have your work cut out for you."

Bess didn't look thrilled.

"Great," George said. "I could use some exercise."

"What about me?" Ned asked. "When do I get started?"

"You'll talk to Mr. du Roque tonight, at the awards dinner," Jason said. "He'll fill you in."

Jason reached into a large side pocket of his jacket and pulled out a sheaf of papers. "I've got maps of the institute grounds; Rockport, the nearest town; and the surrounding area for each of you," he said, passing them out. "I don't want to alarm you," he continued, "but there are a few things you should know before you go wandering around on your own."

Nancy folded her arms across her chest. "What things?" she asked.

Jason frowned. "Well, the institute has experienced some budget cuts recently and has had to reduce the number of guards patrolling the grounds. Since we're practically right in town, and open to the ocean, we're not very well protected. If someone wants to get onto the grounds, he can do it. Those of us who work with the animals and in the lab are careful about locking up when we leave at the end of the day. But the animals are more vulnerable than we'd like them to be."

"Have you told Mr. du Roque that you think the cuts in security are unwise?" Nancy asked.

Jason laughed a short, unpleasant laugh. "Unfortunately, talking to Arman du Roque is like talking to a brick wall. Don't get me wrong," he added hastily. "I like the man. I just don't always agree with him. Anyway, there's one more thing you should know before I take Ned over to the mansion."

When Jason paused, Nancy glanced at her friends. She was sure they were thinking the same thing she was—that they were about to hear something that could spoil their fun for the week.

"Go on," Ned urged.

"For the past three months the institute's been harassed by a group of radical animal rights people who call themselves Sea Friends Forever." Jason looked as if he was about to lose his temper. "They're opposed to our research and to the sea animal performances we give twice a day during tourist season. They say that keeping wild creatures, like dolphins, in captivity, is wrong. No, actually, they say it's cruel."

"And what has this group done?" Nancy asked.

"Well, don't tell du Roque—or Michael Putnam, the institute's director—I told you, but we've had a series of incidents, mostly vandalism and sabotage." Jason paused. "It doesn't matter so much what they've done as what they might do. I'm worried that someone's going to get hurt because of their pranks. Just keep your eyes open, okay?"

"Not a very smart time to cut back on security, is it?" Nancy said.

"Absolutely not. And the real problem is that we have no definite proof that Sea Friends Forever is responsible for the trouble. They've never claimed responsibility, but everything points to them." Suddenly Jason smiled. "Enough doom and gloom," he said. "Ned, let's get you to du Roque's. And I'll see the rest of you at the awards dinner later."

"You bet," Bess said. "We're looking forward to it."

"Yeah." George grinned. "I just *love* rubber chicken."

Chapter

Two

REady or not, here we come," Bess said as she, Nancy, and George climbed the steps of the museum that evening.

"I can't believe you made it over here in those things!" George exclaimed, looking at Bess's stiletto-heeled black satin shoes. "And people say you're not athletic," she added with a grin. George wore a black crepe evening pants suit with bold silver jewelry.

"Thank you, George," Bess said. "I'm glad someone appreciates my talent."

Nancy laughed. "You both look great. Bess, that dress is stunning." Nancy admired her friend's ankle-length black sheath. "I feel kind of left out, being the only one not in black," she added.

"Left out?" George said. "More like *stand*

out. No one is going to see Bess or me with you standing next to us."

"Well, I certainly hope that's not true!" Bess cried. "I mean, Nancy, you *do* look wonderful—dark green is definitely one of your best colors—but I'd like to be noticed, too!"

Nancy took an arm of each of her friends. "Let's go inside."

As the three girls entered the museum lobby, several men, all in tuxedos, turned to them. Nancy knew she looked good. Her strawberry blond hair was swept up in a loose french twist. Her dark green satin dress with the fitted bodice and full, short skirt suited her perfectly.

One of the young men broke away from his group and came over to Nancy, Bess, and George.

"Hello," he said, bowing slightly from the waist. He was tall and thin. His expression was animated, and his smile managed to be both goofy and incredibly charming. In one hand he held a cocktail napkin on which sat an appetizer-size pizza.

"Hello," the three girls said at once. Nancy laughed. "We didn't plan that, really."

The young man laughed easily. "Whatever you say. My name is Dennis. I'm the head tour guide at the institute and, for the preseason, supervisor of the volunteer workers."

"Well, then," Nancy said, "you'll have the pleasure of working with the three of us. I'm Nancy, and these are my friends Bess and George. We're volunteers for the week."

Dennis acted slightly puzzled. "Excuse me if I say the wrong thing," he said, "but I thought the volunteers weren't invited to this shindig."

Nancy laughed. "You're right. But we're friends of Ned Nickerson, the Emerson College student who won the scholarship at the institute. We were invited as his guests."

"Nancy, especially," Bess added. "Ned is Nancy's boyfriend."

"And here he comes now," George added.

"Hi," Ned said. "I thought you'd never get here." He put an arm around Nancy's shoulders and kissed her cheek.

"Ned, this is Dennis. He's the head tour guide at the institute," Nancy explained.

"And our boss," George added.

Ned shook Dennis's hand. "Ned," Dennis said, "you're a lucky man. You're here with the most beautiful woman in the room. Well," he added, turning to Bess and George, "one of the *three* most beautiful women in the room."

George rolled her eyes and laughed. "Dennis, why don't we go get some of those little pizzas? I'm so hungry I'm tempted to steal that one out of your hand."

He nodded to Nancy and said, "We start work bright and early tomorrow morning, so don't stay up too late."

"We won't," Bess replied. "I'm going to find Jason. See you later."

Ned stood silently, staring at George and Dennis as they walked away.

"What's the matter?" Nancy asked.

"Nothing. Except I don't really like that Dennis very much. He seems . . . I don't know, too slick for his own good, maybe."

Nancy grinned and tucked her arm through Ned's. "Don't go getting jealous on me," she said. "Dennis is harmless, I'm sure. I thought he was kind of nice."

Ned shrugged. "If you like his type. Well, I've got to get up to the dais," Ned said, nodding toward the front of the room. "See you later?" he said, kissing Nancy on the nose.

Nancy found her way to her table. She was joined by Bess, George, Jason, and Dennis. During dessert the speeches began. Arman du Roque spoke eloquently about the founding of the institute. Michael Putnam, the director of the institute, followed du Roque. Putnam stressed the importance of supporting a private institution. After Putnam, a woman named Lynn Harris, who was introduced as the head trainer, spoke briefly. Nancy found her unpretentious and obviously devoted to her job and her animals. Finally Ned and the recipients of other awards were officially recognized, and the program was over.

Ned joined Nancy. "Nan, I want to introduce you to Arman du Roque," he said as they made their way to the head table. Arman du Roque was standing and greeting guests as they passed his table.

"Mr. du Roque," Ned began, "this is Nancy Drew."

"What a pleasure, Miss Drew," du Roque responded warmly, shaking Nancy's hand. His hair was an unruly shock of white; his face was deeply lined, probably from years of exposure to sun and cold and wind. Although Arman du Roque had made his reputation as a man of business, Nancy thought he looked like someone who would be more comfortable outdoors than in the boardroom.

"The pleasure is mine," Nancy said. "What a wonderful gift you've given all of us with the institute."

"Thank you," du Roque said. He chuckled. "I have to tell you, though, I didn't set up the institute with the public as my first priority—it was actually for myself."

"I don't understand, sir," Nancy said.

"You see, I devoted most of my life to carrying on the family business. Then one day I woke up and realized that for all of my financial success, I wasn't happy. My wife had died; my children had grown bored with their old father and had never been interested in the family business. I couldn't even say that I blamed them. I, too, was bored with lumber. So I thought about what I might *like* to do with the rest of my life."

"And what was that?" Ned prodded.

Du Roque clasped his hands before him. "Well, in college I studied marine biology, and since I've always loved the ocean, I decided to dedicate my resources to establishing a place where scientists could study marine life. I also wanted people from the community to be able to learn about creatures such as dolphins up close."

Du Roque cleared his throat, then continued. "People think of me as a philanthropist, but I think of myself as a selfish old man. Every time I watch one of our dolphins leap, my heart leaps with it."

Just then Michael Putnam tapped du Roque on the shoulder and whispered to him. Du Roque turned to Nancy and Ned and excused himself, then headed off to mingle with the other guests.

Nancy and Ned joined Bess and Jason in a corridor lined with photographs. "Nancy, Ned," Jason called. "Come here. I want to show you something." Jason pointed to a photograph of a trainer putting a dolphin through its paces for a cheering audience. "If we had more photos like this on display, instead of photos like *this*"—Jason pointed to another photograph of two laboratory scientists intently studying something under a microscope—"the institute might become more profitable."

"What do you mean?" Bess asked.

"I mean that if du Roque allowed us to spend more money and energy on improving the commercial aspects of the institute, we could support ourselves not only with contributions but also from things like ticket sales. As it is, we don't attract enough visitors in one season to keep the aquarium's performance area open and running for one week."

"Where does the money go?" Nancy asked.

Jason's ice blue eyes flashed. "What money there is goes to support research. That's not wrong, but we'll never survive if the institute is only thought of as a dusty little think tank. We have to promote our commercial value, too."

Ned shrugged. "Sounds reasonable to me."

"It is," Jason continued, "but du Roque

doesn't agree. And neither does Lynn." Jason looked at each of the group in turn. "Did you know that one of our dolphins, Chelsea, gave birth to an albino baby recently?"

Nancy shook her head.

"Whitecap's birth is a major event. Albino dolphins are very rare. He could be a huge attraction for the institute. But Putnam wasn't allowed to publicize his birth. Not even a press announcement." Jason thrust his hands into his pants pockets and scowled.

"Jason, do I hear you grousing again?" A small woman with an engaging grin and short salt-and-pepper hair joined them. Nancy recognized her as Lynn Harris, the head trainer.

Jason unfolded his arms and stood straighter. "Oh, hi, Lynn. Nice speech you gave."

"Thanks," she said, and turned to Ned. "I've met Ned, but I haven't met the rest of you."

Nancy introduced herself and Bess.

"Well," Lynn said, "you'll have to excuse Jason. Sometimes he forgets this isn't Sea World. Rocky Isle is a small research organization with an excellent reputation, and an occasional dolphin show. The institute is also an important part of the community. And the community appreciates us just the way we are," she finished.

Jason's eyes flashed. "That's where you're wrong, Lynn," he argued. "The community is losing its faith in us, and if we lose community support . . ." Jason shook his head. "Look, I'm sorry. This isn't the time to be having this argument. I'm going to circulate and press some flesh."

Jason walked off, and when he was out of earshot, Lynn smiled. "Jason Kalb is one of the best young trainers I've ever worked with," she said. "He's smart, and he's passionate about the animals." Lynn sighed. "In spite of his complaining, I believe he really loves the institute. I just don't think he knows what's best for it."

Nancy smiled noncommittally. To her, Jason's concerns sounded completely valid. Still, she didn't know enough about the institute's financial situation to judge whether Jason's ideas for change were good or not.

The group began to drift farther along the corridor.

Nancy stopped to look at a photograph of Lynn and Matt Folton, the star of an old television series called *Sea Lives*. "When did you meet Matt Folton?" Nancy asked Lynn.

Lynn smiled. "That picture is from a former life. It was taken years ago, long before Matt decided that training dolphins was the same as abusing dolphins. I met him on the set of *Sea*

Lives, during the show's last season. I was working as a consultant and expert on dolphin behavior. Matt and I became friends. Ironically, it was through me that he got really interested in dolphins. It wasn't long before Matt quit the show and became an animal rights activist—and stopped being my friend."

"That's too bad," Nancy said.

Lynn sighed. "Yes, it is. I try to respect other people's opinions, but it's hard when someone has no respect for yours. Friendships can't survive in that environment."

A commotion from the main room interrupted Lynn. "What's going on?" she asked, nervously putting a hand to her throat.

"Let's find out," Nancy said. "Come on, Ned." Nancy and Ned took off for the main room ahead of Lynn and Bess. They found Dennis and George silently watching a group of about ten people in handmade dolphin costumes that masked their faces. The demonstrators marched through the double doors into the dining room. They pushed their way through the guests, yelling angrily and waving signs that read, Set the Dolphins Free and Dolphins Aren't Circus Performers!

"What are they doing?" George whispered.

Dennis's face was dark with fury. "Causing trouble, that's what," he said angrily. As he started to move toward the protesters, George grabbed his arm.

"Wait," she said. "See what they do."

George had just finished speaking when two of the people pointed at Michael Putnam, who was standing as if nailed to the floor.

As the protesters approached the director, they pulled plastic bags full of a bloody substance from inside their costumes and tossed the contents in Michael Putnam's face.

Chapter
Three

A COLLECTIVE GASP went up as the bloody mess dripped from Putnam's face onto his shoulders and chest.

"This is outrageous!" Dennis cried. His voice seemed to break a spell that had kept the other guests paralyzed, because suddenly there was movement everywhere. The protesters turned and ran out.

From all corners of the room, Nancy heard panicked whispering.

She turned to Bess, who had joined the group with Lynn. "Bess, call the police."

"Right," she said, and ran off.

"I'll check on Putnam and du Roque," Ned said.

Nancy turned to Dennis. "Dennis, you stay

here and wait for the police. George, come with me."

George nodded and followed Nancy as she raced across the room and through the double doors. When they reached the front steps of the building, they halted. The protesters had vanished. They couldn't have taken off in cars because there was no engine noise.

"I'll head down the driveway toward the town to see if I can spot them," Nancy said.

"And I'll take off toward the mansion and cover as much of the estate as I can," George said.

"George, be careful," Nancy warned her friend. "Remember what Jason told us about the lack of security. If you run into one of the protesters, just identify him or her. Don't put yourself in danger."

George agreed. "If there had been proper security in the first place, the protesters would never have made it into the building. You be careful, too, Nancy."

Nancy nodded. "I will." She ran as quickly as she could in heels along the main driveway toward the town. In a few minutes she reached the institute's main gate and turned onto the town's major thoroughfare. The closer she got to the center of town, the better the sidewalks were lit. Nancy kept her eyes open for clues.

She came upon an elderly man, cane in hand, strolling along the street. "Excuse me, sir," she said as she reached him, her breath coming hard. "I know this sounds crazy, but have you seen anyone wearing a dolphin costume pass this way?"

The old man stopped and looked at her. "I saw them," he blurted out. "They almost knocked me over, tearing along the sidewalk as if they were being chased by ghosts."

Nancy touched the old man's arm. "Where did they go? Did you recognize any of them?" she asked.

The man shook his head. "No. I didn't see them go anywhere once they were past me. Didn't see any faces, either."

Nancy sighed. "Thank you for your help. I'm sorry to have bothered you."

She ran on. In a moment she was passing through the deserted village green and heading for the marina.

On one of the piers, Nancy spotted a group of fishermen standing in a tight clump, talking. "Excuse me," she said, approaching them. No one acknowledged her.

Nancy cleared her throat and tried again, this time a bit louder. "Excuse me!"

Conversation ceased and the men turned to look at her.

"This might sound odd," Nancy began,

"but have you seen anyone dressed as a dolphin pass by here?"

There was a moment of silence, during which the men carefully took in Nancy's satin dress and her hair, which had come out of its pins and was hanging around her face and neck. And then, one by one, they grinned.

Great, Nancy thought. They probably think I'm a refugee from some wild party.

"Well, have you?" she demanded.

One man shook his head. "No, young lady, we haven't." Though he seemed to be speaking for them all, Nancy looked expectantly at the others in the group, but no one else said a word.

"Thanks, anyway," Nancy said brightly, trying to muster some dignity as she turned and walked back toward the village green. She could hear chuckling from behind her as she walked. Well, she thought, either they really didn't see the protesters or they're in some sort of conspiracy with them.

Nancy reached the main thoroughfare and headed back toward the institute. This time she saw no one on the sidewalk, so she concentrated on looking for anything the protesters might have dropped that would help to identify them. She was not really expecting to find anything when she spied a piece of paper stuck in the lower branches of a shrub. Nancy moved to the inside edge of the sidewalk and bent down to retrieve what turned out to be a brochure.

She made her way to the nearest streetlamp to read the brochure.

"Bingo!" Nancy said as she saw the Sea Friends Forever logo on the front cover. There were a number of grotesque photos of animals being mistreated. Nancy turned in distaste from a particularly horrible one and flipped to the back cover.

The photo there was even worse. It was of a smiling Arman du Roque petting the head of a dolphin. A big red X had been printed over his head. And across the X there was one word: "Dead."

By the time Nancy returned to the museum, she was cold and disappointed. She'd come up with nothing more substantial than an inflammatory brochure, dropped, more than likely, by one of the demonstrators as the group made its escape. Still, Nancy would give it to the police as proof that members of Sea Friends Forever were a potential danger to Arman du Roque and the institute.

"Nancy!" someone called, breaking her train of thought. Nancy spun around to see George a few feet behind her, just entering through the double doors.

"Did you find anything?" Nancy asked as George joined her.

"Nothing really. A few footprints. What about you?" George asked.

"Just this." She showed George the brochure.

George whistled low. "Du Roque could be in real danger," she observed.

"I know. That's why I'm giving this to the police. I'm afraid Mr. du Roque would just shrug it off as being meaningless."

"You may be right," George said.

Nancy and George entered the large room in which the awards dinner had been held. George went off to find Ned, while Nancy stopped for a moment to survey the scene. The police were interviewing guests while Michael Putnam, who had removed his soiled dinner jacket and shirt, stood in his tuxedo pants and a Rocky Isle Marine Institute T-shirt, a towel draped around his neck. Even from a distance of several feet, Nancy could see he was still furious.

"What kind of world is this," he asked a police officer who stood with him, pen and pad in hand, "when people can force their way into a private affair and harass the guests?"

Nancy walked toward Putnam and the police officer. "Excuse me, Mr. Putnam, Officer," she said.

"What is it?" Putnam said shortly.

"I ran into town to see if I could find the protesters. One elderly man had seen them, but he couldn't identify them because they had shoved past him so quickly. On the way back to the institute, I did find this." Nancy showed the brochure to the men.

"Propaganda," Putnam said angrily. "Ridiculous."

Nancy handed the brochure to the police officer. "I still think it's worth taking a look at. Especially the back cover."

Nancy watched as the police officer's eyes widened. He then handed the brochure to Putnam. "Miss Drew," the officer said, "if you discover anything else that might be of help, please let us know."

"I will, Officer," Nancy said. "Good night, Mr. Putnam. I'm sorry the event was spoiled."

Putnam stared at the brochure, distracted, as he dismissed Nancy with a quick good night.

"Well," du Roque was saying to Ned, Bess, and George when Nancy joined them. "Maybe I should hire additional security guards."

"With all due respect, du Roque," a familiar voice said, "no amount of paid security can protect us from the obsessions of this group."

Nancy was surprised to see that Putnam had followed her.

"I'm afraid they won't quit until they've shut down the institute," he continued. "However," he added, with a wry smile, "now is not the time to discuss this. I'm going home to wash off the stench of fish guts. I'll see you all tomorrow."

"Yes, good night, Michael," du Roque said. He turned back to Nancy and her friends. "Can I offer you a ride to the administration building? I'm afraid you'll have to walk to your cabin from there."

"That would be great, Mr. du Roque," Nancy answered.

Du Roque led Nancy, Ned, Bess, and George out of the museum to his car.

As they began the short drive to the administration building, du Roque sighed. "We've had a lot of trouble lately, and though we have no definite proof, I'm beginning to believe that the Sea Friends are behind the vandalism as well as behind tonight's disaster."

"What kind of vandalism are you talking about, Mr. du Roque?" Nancy asked. She remembered that Jason had mentioned trouble, but he hadn't given them any specific examples of vandalism.

"Well, just last week one of the lab's newest computers was destroyed." Du Roque shook his head. "The cost of replacing it is not in the budget. Yet without it our work can't go on."

"What else has happened?" Ned asked, leaning toward the front seat.

"Let's see. Our phone lines—those for the lab, the museum, and the administrative offices—were cut one night. That wasn't expensive to repair, but it certainly was a nuisance."

"Has anyone been hurt?" George asked.

Du Roque swung into the drive of the administration building and stopped the car. He turned sideways in his seat. "No, unless you count Putnam's pride being injured tonight." Du Roque chuckled, and Nancy was glad to see he had a sense of humour.

"And Sea Friends Forever has never claimed responsibility for any of these incidents?" Nancy asked.

"No, though we do get hundreds of postcards a week from their members, protesting our work. Before tonight, we've never had to call in the police."

"That was my idea," Nancy said. "I'm sorry if it went against a policy."

"It didn't," du Roque said. "To be honest, I've accepted the advice of Michael Putnam on such things. He's always suggested that we handle the matters ourselves."

Ned frowned. "And how do you do that?" he asked.

"By ignoring the vandalism and not retaliating," du Roque said. "I suppose Michael hoped that if we didn't react violently against Sea Friends Forever they would just go away."

"Mr. du Roque," Ned said, "Nancy has had a lot of experience investigating criminal actions, and she's solved dozens of difficult cases. I'm sure she could help you and the institute with this one."

"I'm not sure exactly what I could do for you, but I'd be happy to try." Nancy thought of the brochure she'd found in the bushes outside the institute and of the danger to Mr. du Roque it suggested. She had to help.

"Thank you, Nancy, Ned," du Roque answered. "I'd be grateful for your help. But I would ask that we keep the arrangement a secret from Lynn, Michael, Jason, and Dennis. They're all working hard to get the institute ready for the season opening in two weeks. I want them to concentrate on that, not on these security problems. The truth is," he added, "I do believe that someone is trying to shut down the institute. And I'm afraid someone is going to get hurt—or worse—in the process."

Chapter

Four

"THAT WAS SCRUMPTIOUS," Bess said, patting her stomach and grinning.

George laughed. "Yeah, one benefit of hard labor is that you can tell yourself it's okay to eat lots of great food—to keep up your strength."

"Right," Nancy added as they left the cafeteria shortly after 7:00 A.M. "Now all we have to do is perform enough hard labor to work off those pancakes!"

"Don't forget the sausage," Bess said, jumping off the porch to the ground.

Nancy, Bess, and George headed toward the water and the dock where the institute kept its boats. There they were to meet Dennis and the other volunteers to get their assignments for the day. Dressed in jeans, heavy sweaters, and mud boots, Nancy and her friends were ready for a day of outdoor labor.

"Remember, guys," Nancy said as they approached the water, "we promised Mr. du Roque we'd keep our investigation secret. So get as much information as you can, but don't blow our cover."

"You can count on us," George said, pulling on her gloves.

Nancy smiled as she spotted Dennis waving to them.

"Good morning," Dennis said warmly. "I hope you got a good night's sleep and ate a hearty breakfast. You can get mighty hungry out there on the ocean!"

George laughed. "We did both," she said.

"And you?" Nancy asked.

"Yes, to both, too," Dennis answered.

Nancy noted that Dennis had obviously decided not to spread the news of the protest at the banquet and was prepared to get on with the day's work.

"Let me introduce you to the rest of our team," Dennis said. "Nancy, Bess, George, this is Jenny Sutherland and Colleen Barnes. They're both juniors at Rockport High. This is their first preseason with us—but we hope not their last."

Dennis smiled so dazzlingly at the two girls

that Nancy didn't know how they'd have the strength to resist volunteering year after year.

"Hi," Nancy said, trying to hide a grin. "I hope you're looking forward to this as much as we are."

"Oh, yes!" Jenny cried.

"Absolutely," Colleen added.

Nancy noticed that neither of them took their eyes off Dennis as they spoke. Well, maybe they would be so preoccupied with Dennis that they'd talk openly about the town's opinion of the institute. After Jason's hints regarding the town losing respect for Rocky Isle, and Nancy's own disappointing experience with the fishermen the night before, she was sure there was something important to be discovered.

"And this is Evan White," Dennis went on, turning away from his teenage worshipers. "He's a former resident of Rockport who now lives in Mountainside, a small town about an hour from here."

Nancy noticed that Evan didn't seem to find Dennis warm and charming at all. In fact, Evan seemed uncomfortable enough to take off at any moment.

"Okay," Dennis said, "and everyone knows who I am—Dennis Markwood, head tour guide and preseason slave driver extraordinaire." He took some papers out of his jacket pocket and waved them triumphantly. "I've got our first assignment here—we'll have to take a boat down the coast a bit—and I'm responsible for making sure you get the job done. So remember, whatever I say, do *not* take it personally."

Jenny and Colleen giggled manically as they all boarded the *Crawdad,* a large, slightly beat-up fishing boat, and put on life jackets.

A few minutes later the captain had the boat chugging toward the cleanup team's first destination. Nancy observed the coastline as they moved along. "Isn't it beautiful?" she said to Dennis, who had taken the seat next to her. "The coastline is so rocky and wild."

Dennis smiled. "Yes, it's incredibly romantic, isn't it?"

Nancy shook her head slightly and smiled. "Uh, if you think that sort of thing is romantic, I guess it is," she answered.

Dennis smiled again. "Okay, everyone, we're almost there."

A few minutes later the captain cut the *Crawdad*'s engine and dropped anchor. They were in front of a small patch of beach strewn with pine branches, seaweed, and other natural debris.

"Wow," George said. "Now I see what Jason meant when he said the trails and coastline get messy during the winter!"

"Hey, how are we supposed to get to the beach?" Bess asked.

"In the dinghy, of course," Dennis said. "Come on, last one overboard is a rotten egg."

One by one, the crew members climbed over the gunwale of the *Crawdad* with rakes and bags hoisted over their heads. The dinghy made two trips before they were all ashore.

Once there, Nancy decided to work beside Jenny to see if she could learn anything more about Rockport's relationship with the institute and with Sea Friends Forever. Evan, she noticed, had chosen to work apart from the rest of them. George was near Dennis, and Bess had cornered Colleen.

"So how's Rockport High?" Nancy asked as she began to rake big clumps of seaweed.

Jenny tossed her long dark braid over her shoulder. "Great. My boyfriend, Tim, is the captain of the basketball team. They did really well this year."

Jenny chatted about school and the track team, of which she was a member. When she was quiet, Nancy asked, "How do your parents feel about your volunteering at Rocky Isle this week? I mean, I've heard some animal rights groups aren't exactly thrilled with what the institute is doing. Are your parents worried about the trouble the groups are causing?"

Jenny tossed her braid again and started to

talk. "My parents don't care much either way about what's going on at Rocky Isle. But, yeah, a lot of people do. I mean, everyone in town knows that some weird group called Sea Friends Forever is after Mr. du Roque."

"How do they know it's Sea Friends Forever?" Nancy asked. "And how do they know the group is after du Roque?"

Jenny shrugged. "About a month ago there were articles in our local newspaper, the *Rockport Gazette,* about animal rights groups. Mr. du Roque was interviewed. He was asked if Rocky Isle had ever been, you know, threatened by a radical group. I'm pretty sure he mentioned Sea Friends Forever. But I can't remember what he said about them."

"So," Nancy asked, "do you think anyone in Rockport is actually a member of Sea Friends Forever?"

Jenny stood up straight and shook her head. "No way. Rockport is so small that everybody knows everybody else's business. If someone in Rockport was involved with Sea Friends Forever, we'd all know about it."

Nancy shrugged. "Okay, but let's say that Sea Friends Forever makes its members agree not to tell anyone about the group's activities. Some of the stuff they do is illegal. Don't you think it's possible that they'd establish a code of silence?"

Jenny frowned, as if mulling over this idea. "Weeeelll . . ." she said. "Rockport is small, but my mother always says we have a habit of ignoring what we don't want to see. Like, for instance, the tourists. We make a lot of our money from fishing, but we also make a lot of it from tourists. All kinds of strangers come through Rockport in the summer, and we ignore them as much as possible. An escaped convict, with his picture plastered all over TV, could probably walk right down Main Street without any of us recognizing him."

Jenny worked silently for a while, and Nancy thought she'd try a slightly different set of questions. If most of Rockport's residents were as uninterested in strange goings-on as Jenny seemed to think they were, no wonder the fishermen Nancy had met the night before could tell her nothing about the protesters. Nancy filled and tied another debris bag and added it to the pile the crew was making close to where the boat was anchored. When she returned, she said to Jenny, "So, what do *you* think of Arman du Roque?"

"Well," Jenny answered, "I don't know him personally, but I've seen him around, and he seems like a guy who really cares about animals. I wouldn't be here if I didn't think Rocky Isle was a good place. But I know that not everyone in Rockport agrees with me."

"What do you mean?" Nancy asked.

"Well, back when Rocky Isle was being built, there was a lot of talk about how it would provide jobs for the townspeople. I remember my brother was just graduating from high school and was hoping for a job here. Also, a lot of people thought Rocky Isle would bring in more tourist traffic." Jenny shrugged. "We might ignore the tourists, but that doesn't mean we don't want them here!"

"What happened?" Nancy asked.

"Rocky Isle hasn't produced many jobs for locals, and now the rumor is that the staff isn't getting paid. Also, the institute hasn't brought in half as many tourists as we thought it would. It's got nothing but two little dolphin shows a day. People don't seem interested in the scientific stuff. And Rocky Isle is attracting protesters. Most people in Rockport don't like what the radical groups stand for, because a lot of us fish for a living. But I'll bet some people in town wouldn't mind if Sea Friends Forever managed to close down Rocky Isle."

"That's too bad," Nancy said. "Hasn't the du Roque family done a lot for the community over the years?"

Nancy and Jenny dragged the last of their bags filled with debris over to the general pile.

"Yeah," Jenny said, "the du Roque family helped build the high school and the library.

But now they can't even afford to pay a full-time maintenance staff for the institute." Jenny smiled. "That's why we're here, I guess!"

"I guess," Nancy agreed. "Come on. Let's get back to the boat."

Nancy and Jenny joined the others as they got into the dinghy and rowed back to the boat. Dennis told them that another boat would be by later to collect the bags.

Nancy rejoined Bess and George in the bow. "So," Bess asked, "get any good information? Looked like you two were having a gab fest."

Nancy smiled. "Well, I learned a lot about the relationship between the town and the institute. I'd like to talk to Jason when we get back and see what he can add."

Bess sighed. "You and me both! I'm so cold right now. Just thinking of Jason and Ned working in that nice warm aquarium makes me envious."

The *Crawdad* made another stop at a picnic area, where the crew spent an hour cleaning up more debris. By the time they boarded again, they were exhausted but determined to keep going.

They picked up their brown-bag lunches and found deck space to sit while they dug into their meals. Nancy was finishing a cup of luke-warm coffee when her attention was caught by an elegant motorboat approaching the *Crawdad* on a parallel course.

"What a beautiful boat," she said, nudging George.

"Yeah. It's big," George answered. "There are about ten people on deck."

Bess waved jauntily and called, "Ahoy!"

Dennis came and stood beside Nancy. "I've never seen that boat before," he murmured. "I wonder . . ."

Just then a large white banner with black writing was unfurled over the rail of the boat. It read, Free the Dolphins.

Dennis made a sound of disgust and turned away. The boat was almost alongside the *Crawdad* now. Nancy was startled when one of the passengers raised a gun and aimed it straight at the *Crawdad*.

Chapter
Five

HIT THE DECK," Nancy yelled just as the *Crawdad* was rocked by a tremendous *boom*.

Thick black smoke hung low over the boat. She held one hand over her mouth and crawled toward a cylindrical object that lay on the deck.

When she reached it, Nancy grabbed the object. It was the spent casing of a smoke bomb, the kind that could be fired from a signal flare gun.

Nancy got up on her knees and squinted through the clearing smoke. The motor boat was gone, and she hadn't heard it speed away. She turned toward the other crew members. Dennis was on his feet, but George was kneeling beside Colleen, her arm around the shaking girl. Jenny and Evan were rubbing their eyes. Bess was brushing soot off her clothes.

"Is everyone all right?" Nancy asked.

"We're fine," Bess answered. "Just a little surprised."

"And angry!" Dennis declared. "I will not have my crew endangered by those crazy people!"

"Dennis, I don't think they were trying to hurt us as much as scare us." Nancy showed him the spent smoke-bomb casing. "And we can't be positive the gun was fired by members of Sea Friends Forever."

Dennis scowled. "No, but we can be pretty sure. Typical hit-and-run cowards. They have no problem attacking, but they won't stick around to fess up or talk. We don't even know what the group is protesting, exactly. And they wonder why nothing ever gets resolved!"

"That's true," Jenny said. "Remember that forum sponsored by the *Rockport Gazette* about two months ago?"

Dennis laughed bitterly. "Yeah. Members from all sides of the issue were supposed to meet and talk openly."

"What happened?" Nancy prompted.

"No one from Sea Friends Forever made an appearance. Well, that's not true, exactly. About fifteen minutes after the forum was scheduled to begin, a pizza delivery guy walked into the meeting with ten pizzas to be delivered to 'the warden of Rocky Isle.' Someone had ordered the pizzas in the name of the warden, meaning du Roque, of course."

"That stunt could only have made things worse," George said.

"She's right," Bess added. "Sea Friends Forever and other animal rights groups might have some valid points. But hostile and childish actions totally turn people off."

Evan, who until now hadn't said a word, cleared his throat. Dennis turned sharply to him. "Do you have something to say, Evan?" he asked.

Nancy couldn't help but notice that Dennis's tone had taken on a harder, slightly sarcastic edge as he spoke to Evan.

"Uh, yes," Evan said, shifting from one foot to the other. "I think the members of Sea Friends Forever have a right to state their views," he said hurriedly.

Dennis folded his arms across his chest. "Let me ask you this, Evan. We were victims of a malicious prank just a few moments ago. Did that seem constructive to you?"

Evan's face turned red. "No," he said quickly. "No, I'm not saying that shooting a smoke bomb was a good idea. Someone could have gotten hurt. All I'm saying is that I can understand how people might think that containing a wild animal is cruel."

Before Nancy could intervene, Dennis spoke again. "If that's how you feel, then why are you working for the institute?"

Nancy glanced at George and Bess, each of whom briefly caught her eye. Then she focused on the two young men.

Evan seemed to have gained a little confidence. When he spoke, his voice was stronger. "Listen, Dennis, I wouldn't be volunteering for the institute if I didn't believe that Mr. du Roque cares about the animals studied here. I know he spends a lot of money on research—a lot more money than he spends on beefing up the entertainment value of Rocky Isle."

Evan looked at Nancy, as if for support. She nodded in encouragement.

"But there's another side to the story. Do you know what happens to animals that rely on echolocation when they're confined for prolonged periods of time?"

Evan scanned the faces of the crew. If Dennis knew the answer, he made no attempt to share it. His expression remained grim. Nancy shook her head.

Evan continued. "These animals can go mad. The signals they send out to communicate with others of their species bounce off the walls of their tanks and return to them. It's as if they're imprisoned in an echo chamber. That sounds cruel to me."

"So," Jenny asked slowly, "you *agree* with Sea Friends Forever?"

Evan sighed with frustration. "No, that's not what I'm saying." He paused. "I guess what I'm trying to say is that it seems to me there are more than two sides to this issue—and neither the institute nor Sea Friends is completely right or completely wrong."

When he spoke, Dennis had trouble controlling the anger that threatened to burst loose. "I'm sorry, Evan. I still don't understand why you're working for the institute. I want my team members to be loyal to the cause—not to second-guess everything we do."

"I don't think Evan is second-guessing the institute," Nancy said. "I agree with what he's saying about this particular issue being much too complex to divide into one wrong side and one right side."

"It's the only intelligent way to think about issues like animal rights," George added, challenging Dennis.

"That's right," Evan said. "Look, Dennis, I love the animals at the institute. I do what I can to help the institute continue its studies, even if it means clearing paths so that tourists can come here to watch a daily dolphin show I wish didn't exist." He shoved his hands in his pockets and stared at the deck.

Dennis looked at Evan and then turned and walked off toward the *Crawdad*'s captain. Evan moved to a seat where he could watch the coastline. Jenny and Colleen linked arms and sat near Evan. Nancy beckoned George and Bess to join her.

"Whoa," Bess said. "Dennis sure is devoted to the institute! I mean, he barely listened to Evan. And *he* complains about Sea Friends Forever not communicating well!"

Their conversation was interrupted by Dennis. "We're heading back," he shouted from where he stood beside the captain of the boat. "That sky looks threatening, and I think we've had enough excitement for one day."

"Fine by me," George said.

"Look!" Dennis exclaimed as the girls were about to resume their conversation. Nancy turned to see what Dennis was pointing at out at sea. A humpback whale was just surfacing. Nancy gasped.

"How beautiful!" she cried. Nancy, Bess, and George ran to the rail. Nancy glanced at Dennis and smiled at the awe expressed on his face.

"I've seen that sight hundreds of times," Dennis said, "and it always takes my breath away."

Suddenly several dolphins broke the surface of the water around the whale and then disappeared. Nancy was struck by their incredible grace and by how they looked in open water. She thought of the dolphins back at the institute's aquarium. They were well fed and well loved, but they weren't free. And that was the big difference.

Nancy's reverie was broken by the startling chill of a raindrop falling on her forehead. She hurriedly pulled her hood over her head and hoped the *Crawdad* would reach land soon.

Ned and Jason, staying dry under the awning of an equipment shack, were waiting for the *Crawdad* when the boat docked. Nancy had been so preoccupied with the strange events that had occurred since they arrived at Rocky Isle the day before, she'd almost forgotten that her most important reason for coming to the institute was to spend time with Ned.

"Ahoy thar, matey," Ned called to Nancy. "Did you bring me any buried treasure?"

Nancy jumped onto the dock and ran to her boyfriend. She gave him a big hug and said, "No, but we did bring you an adventure story."

By then George, Bess, and Dennis had joined Nancy, Ned, and Jason. Nancy quickly related the smoke-bomb incident.

When she'd finished, Ned pulled Nancy to him once again. "I'm so glad no one was hurt," he said.

Jason looked at Bess. "Me, too," he added. "But on a lighter note, don't forget we've got a date with Whitecap. I don't like to keep the little guy waiting."

Dennis remained on board to help the captain of the *Crawdad* after arranging to meet his crew later at the aquarium. Jenny, Colleen, and Evan trailed behind Nancy, Ned, the cousins, and Jason.

Before joining the others at the tank in which Whitecap and his mother, Chelsea, were kept, Nancy stopped to call the police to report the smoke-bomb incident. That taken care of, she made her way to where her friends were leaning over the rail of the tank.

"Oh, Nancy," Bess called. "Come see. He's so cute!"

"I think I'm going to die!" Jenny squealed, her hand to her heart.

Ned smiled and made room for Nancy at the rail.

"Hey, little guy," Nancy called. "Jason, can you tell us something about Whitecap and his mom? What kind of dolphins are they?"

"These guys are called Atlantic bottlenose dolphins. You've probably seen the species on TV. They're the ones at most marine parks, the dolphins who perform in shows. They're very intelligent, and they love to have fun. Look out!" Jason ducked as Chelsea jumped out of the water and dived back in with a huge splash.

"Wow," Bess said, shaking water out of her hair. "That was some jump!"

"Yeah," Jason agreed. "Chelsea is quite an athlete. And see how her lower jaw protrudes beyond the upper jaw? That's characteristic of bottlenose dolphins. So is the triangular dorsal fin. These guys are fast, too. They can maintain a speed of sixteen to twenty miles an hour."

"How big do they get?" George asked.

"A lot of them get to be about five hundred pounds. But some weigh as much as fifteen hundred pounds," Jason answered.

"Wow," Ned said. "That's incredible. What do they eat?"

"Fish," Jason answered. "And you know, of course, that dolphins are mammals. They need oxygen in order to live, though the Atlantic bottlenose can remain under water for six or seven minutes."

"How big was Whitecap when he was born?" Nancy asked.

"He was of average size, about three and a half feet long," Jason said. "The mothers give birth to one calf at a time. The gestation period is ten to twelve months. And the baby nurses for over a year."

"Being a mommy dolphin is a big job, isn't it?" Bess crooned to Chelsea.

"Okay, guys, let's give Whitecap a rest," Jason joked. "Anyway, I don't want all this attention to go to his head."

Reluctantly the group broke up—but not before Bess swore Whitecap had smiled at her. Bess, George, Evan, Jenny, and Colleen went to help Dennis repair nets and lines. Nancy promised to catch up with them later. First, though, she wanted to speak with Mr. du Roque.

"Ned, will you come with me?" she asked.

"Sure," he answered. "I need to talk to him about my work, anyway."

"Great. Let's go."

The two set off for the du Roque mansion. As they approached the massive old building, Nancy whistled.

"Wow. I didn't realize how impressive this place was."

Ned grinned. "Yeah, imagine how I feel, staying here as a guest. Especially at night. I keep expecting a valet to ask me if I need help getting undressed!"

"Or a ghost to ask if you want to join him in a romp around the graveyard," Nancy added mischievously.

Ned grabbed Nancy's arm. "Is there really a graveyard on the property?"

Nancy burst out laughing. "I don't know, but if there is, I'll protect you!"

Nancy and Ned reached the front door of the du Roque mansion and rang the bell. They were shown into Arman du Roque's study immediately.

"Nancy, Ned, I'm glad to see you," du Roque said warmly as he rose to greet them. "Please, have a seat."

"Thank you, sir," Nancy said. "I'm afraid I have more unpleasant news to report." Nancy told him as succinctly as she could about the incident with the smoke bomb.

"I informed the police when we got back to shore," she finished. "They said they had no leads on last night's protest at the museum, but they're still on the case. As I am," Nancy added.

Du Roque rubbed his eyes with his right hand. "I don't mind telling you that I'm getting worried," he said. "Someone could have been seriously injured this afternoon."

"But no one was," Nancy reminded him simply. "I'm going to join Dennis and the others now. I'm sure you and Ned have plenty of work to do. Right, Ned?"

Ned sat forward in his chair and spoke briskly. "That's right, Mr. du Roque. We can't let these incidents interrupt the plans for the institute's opening."

Du Roque smiled wanly. "Yes, you're right. Let's get busy."

After an afternoon spent working inch by inch through long lengths of nets, repairing frayed and damaged sections with new bits of rope, Nancy, Bess, and George were more than ready for a hearty dinner.

"My hands are *so* gross," Bess wailed, holding out her work-reddened fingers for Nancy and George to see.

"Yeah," George agreed. "I must have fifteen cuts on my hands. Not to mention the rope burns!"

"Well, no one said this work was going to be easy," Nancy said ruefully.

The three friends entered the cafeteria. As they surveyed the room, Nancy spotted Evan standing alone by the serving table. "I'm going to ask Evan to sit with us," Nancy whispered to her friends. "I'd like to hear more of what he has to say."

Nancy approached Evan and smiled. "Hi," she said. "How about sitting with me over there?" She nodded toward the table at which George and Bess had dropped their jackets.

Evan hesitated, as Nancy had known he would.

"I thought you expressed some very intelligent opinions today on the *Crawdad,*" she continued. "I'd like to hear more."

Evan nodded and took a plate. When they joined George and Bess, they found that Ned and Jason had also settled at the table. "Here, sit next to me," Nancy prompted Evan.

For a few minutes Nancy chattered about herself, hoping to put Evan at ease. She told him about her home in River Heights, about Hannah, about her father, and finally about her relationship with Ned.

It seemed to do the trick. "I've lived in Mountainside for the past seven years," Evan said. "But as Dennis said earlier, I grew up around here. I like Rockport. It's my home. So after college, I decided to come back. I haven't found a job yet, but I majored in marine biology, so I thought I'd do some volunteer work here, get in on the ground floor."

"Sounds like a good idea," Nancy said. "I was talking to Jenny today about what the locals think of the institute and Sea Friends and their battle. Do you think any local people are involved with Sea Friends Forever?" Nancy asked him.

Evan hesitated before speaking. "Well," he said after a moment's pause, "I've read that Sea Friends Forever is a large group, with members and chapters nationwide. But let's face it, because of their tactics, they don't talk much to the press. As far as I know, there could be local members, but if there are, I'm sure they don't go around announcing it."

"You're right," Nancy said. "On the other hand, in a town as small as Rockport, it seems as if people—or at least some people—would know if their neighbors were involved in a secret organization."

Evan suddenly frowned. "You know," he began slowly, "I just remembered something. I didn't think much about it at first, but . . ."

"What is it?" Nancy asked.

Evan turned in his seat to face her and said, "The other day, before I started here at Rocky Isle, I was in the drugstore on Main Street. There was a guy in there. . . . I thought I recognized him from high school. He wasn't a friend of mine," Evan said. "In fact, he was a troublemaker, so I didn't bother to say hello. Anyway, I heard him say something about the party at the museum. He said something about how the boss was going to love it. He and the guy he was talking to laughed and gave each other a high five. Maybe he was talking about what happened at the museum last night." Evan smiled. "I know you're wondering how I found out. Well, I heard about it from a cafeteria worker this morning at breakfast. Don't ask me where *he* heard about it."

"Evan," Nancy said, "I want to find out who's responsible for the vandalism and this afternoon's attack. If it *is* Sea Friends Forever, I want to know who they're using locally to stage the incidents. Would you tell me the name of this guy you saw at the drugstore? I'd like to talk to him."

Evan paled and dropped his fork. "Uh, I don't know if that's such a good idea, Nancy," he said.

"Why not?" Nancy asked, meeting his gaze directly. "You want to know who's behind the attacks, don't you?"

Evan swallowed hard. "Of course. His name is Andy Gergen. I think he still lives with his mother on Cascade Street. Excuse me." Evan stood, picked up his plate and glass, and hurried away.

Nancy turned back to her meal. That was strange, she thought. First, he told me all about Andy Gergen. Then he acted as if he didn't want me to follow up on it. Nancy reasoned that Evan was aware of the many sides of the issue involving the institute but he hadn't decided where he stood.

Nancy sighed and rolled onto her back. She brought her watch with the illuminated dial close to her face and saw that it was 11:30 P.M. It was no use. She couldn't sleep. She'd wanted to talk to Ned after dinner and tell him what she'd learned from Evan, but he'd had to hurry off for a meeting with du Roque.

Nancy sat up in bed. What if she paid a visit to the mansion right now? Ned was probably still awake, maybe even still working.

Resolved, Nancy got out of bed and dressed quickly in her warmest gear. Careful not to wake George and Bess, who were sleeping soundly, she picked up her flashlight.

Nancy stole out of the cabin and breathed deeply. The air was cold but invigorating. After getting her bearings—she could see the twin floodlit towers of the du Roque mansion in the distance—she set out on the correct trail, the flashlight illuminating the ground beneath her feet.

She had been walking for no more than five minutes when a noise startled her—the sound of a twig breaking underfoot. Under a *person's* foot. Nancy stopped and listened hard, but the night was now still.

She walked another few feet, and her heart slammed in her chest. A large figure stepped from behind a tree and trained a high-intensity flashlight beam directly on her face, blinding her.

Chapter

Six

NANCY COULDN'T MOVE. She felt like a deer caught in the headlights of an oncoming car. But the person who loomed not ten feet in front of her stood as still as she did. She ducked her head and raised her hand to shield her eyes in a futile attempt to see more clearly.

A second later Nancy's eyes had adjusted enough to make out a few details. The person was big, probably too big to be a woman. He was wearing a canvas all-weather jacket, probably chosen for camouflage purposes. And the man's face, she saw now, was covered to the eyes by some sort of dark mask.

Nancy leveled a kick at his arm and knocked the flashlight from his hand. She assumed a fighting stance, expecting the man to lunge at her. She was thoroughly surprised when instead of attacking her, he turned off the trail and ran into the woods.

Nancy breathed deeply and retrieved the man's flashlight. She aimed it in the direction he had run, but he was now long gone. Her heart pounding, she briefly examined the flashlight in her hand. It was a heavy piece of equipment, heavier than the average flashlight. Heavier and more powerful than Nancy's own. She would have to turn it over to the police at some point. She'd also check at the hardware and sports equipment stores in town to see if any of them sold this particular brand and model.

Nancy decided she'd better return to her cabin and talk to Ned in the morning. Now she had two stories to tell, and two leads to pursue—Andy Gergen and the flashlight left by the prowler.

Nancy gasped and sat up in bed. "What was that?" she cried.

From her bed across the room, George replied, "Sounded like breaking glass to me. Be careful, everyone. Don't step out of bed without putting on your slippers first."

"I'll get the lights," Bess said.

Nancy heard rapid clomping, a crash, and then a loud "Ow!" In a moment the cabin was flooded with light. Nancy looked at her friend and laughed. Bess had stuck her bare feet in her work boots, then knocked over a chair in her haste to turn on the lights.

Bess scowled. "I don't see anything funny about this. I'm going to have a huge bruise on my shin."

"Sorry, Bess," Nancy apologized. She reached for her slippers and joined George and Bess in the middle of the room.

"Well, whatever broke wasn't in here," George said. "Every window is intact and there's no glass on the floor."

"Let's check the bathroom," Nancy said.

"I'll do it," Bess said, raising her chin. "After all, I'm the only one who was smart enough to put on boots."

Bess clomped toward the cabin's small bathroom and turned on the light. She said nothing but grasped the doorframe tightly.

"Bess?" Nancy asked. "What is it?"

Bess turned toward Nancy and George, her face pale. "The bathroom window is shattered." She stepped aside so Nancy could peer into the room beyond her.

On the bathroom floor, a fist-size rock lay in a pile of broken glass. Attached to the rock with fishing wire were three severed fish heads. One for each of them? Nancy stared at the grisly scene and then crooked a finger at George to come and look.

"There's a note," Nancy said when George had joined her. Gingerly she made her way over to the rock and extricated a small piece of paper from between the rock and fishing wire.

"Gross," Bess said. "I can't believe you touched that mess."

"Well, someone had to," Nancy said, rejoining her friends. Carefully she unfolded the damp, dirty piece of paper.

"What does it say?" George asked grimly.

Nancy read the note aloud: "'Leave Sea Friends Forever alone—or else!'"

"I can't believe this!" Bess said angrily. "When is this going to stop? One of us could have gotten hurt."

Nancy shook her head. "I don't think this was meant to hurt anyone. I think it was meant as a warning, like the smoke bomb." She sighed and checked her watch. "Look, it's almost six o'clock. Let's clean up the bathroom, cover the window, and get dressed. Then we can check for clues outside the cabin before breakfast."

"Right," George said.

Nancy, Bess, and George returned to their cabin after a brief check outside.

"Everyone else is still sleeping, so they must not have seen or heard anything," Bess reported.

"I found some footprints behind the cabin," Nancy said. "Average-size running shoes." She shrugged. "Could belong to a man or a woman. And I have something to tell you guys before we join the others."

Nancy briefly related her encounter with the man on the path. She showed George and Bess the flashlight she'd taken from him.

Bess threw her arms around Nancy and squeezed. "I'm so glad you're all right!"

"Do you think the man you met on the path was the same one who broke the bathroom window?" George asked.

"It's possible," Nancy said, "but the man I saw on the path was really big. The footprints behind the cabin are probably too small to belong to him."

"And," Bess added, "the man on the path might just have been a prowler. You know, someone from town who thought he could break in somewhere on the grounds. Whoever threw that stuff through the window wanted us to know he was a member of Sea Friends Forever."

"Or a supporter of the group," George said.

"Are you going to report the prowler to the police?" Bess asked.

Nancy thought for a moment and then shook her head. "No," she said, "I don't think so. Not yet, anyway. And," she added, "I think we should keep the prowler incident a secret among ourselves."

"You're not going to tell Ned?" George asked.

Nancy laughed. "Okay, you got me there. You know I tell Ned everything."

"Even how Dennis keeps giving you *meaningful* looks?" Bess teased.

Nancy felt her face color. "That's not true," she replied lightly. "Anyway, Dennis is just a flirt."

George raised an eyebrow. "Maybe. But he seems particularly fond of flirting with you."

Nancy ignored the comment and said, "Come on, let's go to breakfast."

"Yeah, I'm starved," Bess said as she grabbed her jacket.

The three friends left the cabin, locked the door, and headed for the cafeteria. Nancy let George and Bess walk together ahead of her. She needed time to think. Who was the man she'd met on the path the night before? And who threw the rock with the fish heads and note? Could it have been the same man? If so, what had he been looking for along the path? Where had he been going? Had he followed her back to the cabin and broken the bathroom window to show Nancy that she hadn't intimidated him earlier that night? That seemed unlikely and a little too risky.

But it did seem likely that the warning was meant specifically for her.

Nancy hurried to catch up with her friends. She couldn't wait to do some serious sleuthing.

The three friends sat drinking coffee and juice and eating French toast with sausage. At another table, Jenny, Colleen, and Evan sat with Dennis. Nancy stole a glance at Dennis. Was he flirting even now? Evan's head was bent over his food, but Jenny was laughing and Colleen's face was flushed. Dennis gestured dramatically—he was probably telling a funny story, Nancy guessed—and then he stared directly at Nancy. She was startled at having been caught looking at him. Dennis didn't seem to mind, though. He smiled slowly and held her glance for a moment before returning to his rapt audience.

"Nancy."

"Huh?" Nancy turned sharply to see Ned standing beside her table. "Oh, hi." She smiled, but Ned didn't return her smile.

"What's wrong?" Bess asked, stuffing a piece of French toast into her mouth.

Just then Jason walked through the doorway, his expression as grim as Ned's.

"Jason, what happened?" Nancy asked.

Jason hesitated long enough for Dennis and the rest of his table to fall silent. Then he said, "Whitecap is missing."

Chapter
Seven

MISSING! What do you mean 'missing'?" Dennis asked.

"Oh, no, the poor little guy!" Bess exclaimed.

Nancy put her hand on Ned's arm. "When did you discover he was gone?"

"Jason did, this morning," Ned answered.

Jason rubbed his hand across his forehead. His voice was low and strained. "When I got to the aquarium pools early this morning, the security gate between the dolphins' indoor tank and the outdoor holding tank was open. Chelsea was in the first tank, alone. The moment I saw her, I knew something was wrong. I ran outside to check the holding tank—it was empty. But the gate to the ocean was closed."

"Sea Friends Forever." Evan spoke up. "It has to be."

"No," Jason said. "That doesn't make sense. If they were trying to free our dolphins, why would they leave the gate to the ocean locked so that Chelsea couldn't escape? The farthest she could go was the outdoor holding tank."

"I agree with Evan," Dennis said, his face a mask of fury. "Any of the other dolphins could probably survive in the open ocean, but Whitecap is too young. He needs his mother. This is the Sea Friends' sick way of proving a point."

"I still say no," Jason argued. "Those people want to save dolphins, not kill them. Separating Whitecap from his mother is too cruel, even for Sea Friends Forever."

Fifteen minutes later Nancy, Lynn Harris, Jason, and Ned stood in the aquarium watching Whitecap's mother, Chelsea, swim restlessly back and forth. Dennis had taken the others off to start gearing up for an intensive search.

"I double-checked the locks on all the tanks," Lynn said, "and as far as I can tell, nothing has been tampered with. The alarm hasn't gone off in the last twenty-four hours.

Except for the gate between the indoor and outdoor tank being open, absolutely nothing is out of place."

"Except Whitecap," Jason murmured.

"It's as if he simply vanished," Lynn added.

Nancy frowned. "Or as if someone who knew his or her way around the aquarium purposely released him," she said. "Leaving the one gate unlocked was only a careless slip."

Lynn shook her head. "No, no way," she said. "I can't believe any of our staff would harm the dolphins. Besides, what motive could a staff member have?"

"Whitecap is our star attraction," Jason said. "An albino dolphin is pretty rare."

"With Whitecap's disappearance, I think we have to talk about all the other strange things that have been going on," Nancy said. She told them about her encounter with the prowler on the path and about the rock with the three severed fish heads and the warning note that someone had thrown through the bathroom window earlier that morning. "No one was hurt in either case," Nancy stressed.

Ned spoke angrily. "Nancy, just because you weren't hurt doesn't mean you couldn't have been."

"Ned's right," Jason added. "We've got a major security breach. Whitecap disappeared between eight-thirty last night and six-thirty this morning. During that same time someone was prowling the grounds and vandalizing the institute's property."

Lynn sighed. "I'll talk to Mr. du Roque about hiring more guards. He'll be devastated when he learns that Whitecap is gone."

"I'll tell him, if you like," Nancy offered. She felt terrible, especially since she had promised Mr. du Roque that she would try to discover the source of the problem and put a stop to the vandalism. But what had she done to keep that promise? Nothing yet. Crimes were happening faster than she had expected, and they were getting progressively more dangerous. It wouldn't be long before someone was hurt. Or worse.

"Nancy, would you talk to him?" Lynn said, laying a hand on Nancy's arm. "I'd really appreciate it. I have so much to do here."

"Ned, let's help Dennis get the gear and boats ready for the search, okay?" Jason asked.

"Sure thing." Ned turned to Nancy. "Please be careful, Nan. Okay?" He kissed her lightly on the cheek.

Nancy smiled. "Okay." She was about to turn back to Lynn when she heard a shrill voice call out.

"Lynn!"

A tall redhead appeared in the doorway.

The woman was gorgeously dressed in a form-fitting hunter green suit with matching high heels. She would be beautiful, Nancy thought, if her face wasn't set in such a bitter, angry expression.

"That's Wendy Zeller," Lynn whispered to Nancy. "Michael's assistant."

Wendy walked up to them and said abruptly, "Michael wants to see you in his office, Lynn. Right away."

The sound of excited voices distracted Lynn from answering immediately. Nancy saw Dennis returning with members of the cleanup crew as well as with a few people Nancy had seen around the institute but had not yet met.

"I'm sorry, Wendy," Lynn said. "But my volunteers are here, and I have a search to organize. Tell Michael I'll speak to him later."

"He'll be furious," Wendy said tightly.

"I know," Lynn said. "Still, I'll take the chance of angering him. Now," she added, "if you'll both excuse me?"

Nancy nodded, and Lynn left the room.

"Without Whitecap, the institute is sunk," Wendy said. "He's our main attraction."

"But I thought the institute didn't rely on entertainment spectacles to support itself," Nancy said.

Wendy shrugged. "That's what du Roque says, but he doesn't know. And certainly he doesn't know what's best for Rocky Isle. He should leave the decisions to the people who know what they're doing." With that, Wendy walked out.

"What's up?"

At the sound of Ned's voice, Nancy turned to find that he and Jason had returned.

"Was that Wendy the Witch I just saw leaving the aquarium?" Jason asked with a scowl.

Nancy nodded.

"Wendy and Putnam were a couple for a long time," Jason told Nancy and Ned. "He dumped her about a year ago, but she still works for him. She's been his assistant for almost ten years."

"Why does she still work at the institute?" Nancy asked.

Jason gave a pained laugh. "Why do any of us?"

Half an hour later Lynn had gathered the entire volunteer crew and the permanent staff members of the institute—from cafeteria workers to lab technicians—on the bleachers. She stood on the floor in front of them, giving instructions for the morning's search.

"Whitecap will probably be hovering near the shore, looking for his mother," she said. As if to reinforce Lynn's comment, Chelsea let out a heartsick cry. Nancy felt tears spring to her eyes. "And hoping to hear his mother calling to him," Lynn added.

George raised her hand. "Lynn, how long do we have? I mean, how long can Whitecap survive on his own?"

"With such a young animal, time is of the essence. Whitecap needs his mother's food and protection. I'd say we have two days tops."

A hush fell over the room as everyone digested this grim information.

Lynn continued. "Everyone will get an assignment. Some of you will be out on boats; others will be searching from the shore. You'll each get a walkie-talkie. I'll stay here to receive your information and give direction. Okay, I want Bess and George to team up with Jason. Dennis, you take . . ."

Lynn finished organizing the search teams, and within a few minutes they were on their way, with the understanding that they would meet again at lunchtime.

Ned turned to Nancy. "I've got to finish some paperwork. I promised Mr. du Roque I'd have it ready for him by noon. I'll join the search this afternoon if Whitecap hasn't been found by then."

Nancy nodded. "I told Lynn I'd tell Mr. du

Roque about Whitecap, so I'd better go now. Walk with me?"

"You were right, Mr. du Roque. The acts of vandalism weren't random at all. Something is going on. And I promise I'll get to the bottom of it."

Nancy had just finished telling Arman du Roque about the prowler she'd encountered on the path the night before; about the broken bathroom window and the fish heads and warning note; and, finally, about Whitecap's disappearance. She'd been considering the possibility of kidnapping since she first heard of the baby dolphin's disappearance, but she hadn't mentioned her suspicion to anyone, not even Mr. du Roque. Better not to worry the staff even more. Better to wait for a ransom note—if this was a kidnapping.

Mr. du Roque put his head in his hands and sighed. "This is much worse than I ever imagined."

The phone rang. After a moment's hesitation du Roque gestured to Nancy. "Would you please answer that for me? Please don't tell whoever's on the line about Whitecap."

Nancy picked up the receiver. "This is Nancy Drew," she said. "I work with Mr. du Roque. . . . It's the police," she silently mouthed to du Roque.

After a few minutes, during which she mainly listened, Nancy hung up.

"Well?" du Roque asked. "Have the police learned anything?"

"Not much, unfortunately," Nancy said. "No one in town will talk about who might have broken up the awards dinner or about who might have been on the boat that fired the smoke bomb. Several boats of the right type were rented out yesterday. The police have questioned the captains of the boats, but none of them noticed anything unusual about their passengers—or so they say. Not one of the boats was rented by an organization—all were leased by individuals."

"Do you think it was wise to tell them about the prowler and the broken window?" du Roque asked nervously.

"I do now," Nancy said. "I had decided not to tell them earlier today, but it's never good to withhold information. Oh, they said they haven't been able to find out where that Sea Friends Forever pamphlet was printed."

Du Roque smiled wearily. "I don't mind telling you, Nancy, that I feel a bit over-whelmed. Whitecap's disappearance is a terrible tragedy. And coming on top of everything else that's happened . . ."

"Please don't give up hope," Nancy said.

"The institute needs a strong leader right now. Don't worry. So far, no one has been hurt."

Du Roque looked at Nancy and smiled wanly. "Except possibly Whitecap. If word of his disappearance gets out, we could lose all of the pledged funding we have raised. And if we have to delay the opening . . ." Du Roque paused. "I might as well say goodbye to the institute."

Chapter

Eight

CASCADE STREET. Nancy checked the address she'd written on her notepad before she left the institute. She'd found only one Gergen listed in the phone book. It had to be Andy's home.

Nancy turned her Mustang into the driveway of number 3060. The porch needed painting, she noticed, and the rocking chairs on either side of the front door were old and rickety.

Nancy took a breath and rang the doorbell. After almost a minute, a young man opened the door.

"Andy?" Nancy said.

He eyed her suspiciously, pushing a lock of long dark hair off his forehead. He wore a black T-shirt and faded jeans. "Do I know you?" he asked.

"No," Nancy replied. "My name is Nancy Drew. May I come in?"

Andy shrugged and stepped back so that Nancy could enter the foyer. He didn't ask her into the living room or into the kitchen to sit.

Nancy folded her arms and said, "What can you tell me about Sea Friends Forever?"

Nancy's blunt question and tone took Andy by surprise. "Wh-what?" he sputtered.

"I said, what can you tell me about Sea Friends Forever?"

"What do you want to know?"

"I'm on a fact-finding mission," she said. "Helping out a friend. Rumor has it that you might know where I can find 'the boss.'"

Andy put up his hands as if to ward off trouble. "Hey," he said, "I don't know who told you that, but it's not true. I don't know anything about them. I think you should go."

"No, I don't think I should," she said, shaking her head. "You see, I have proof that you're associated with Sea Friends Forever and that you were involved in their breaking up the awards dinner at the Rocky Isle Institute museum the other night."

Andy blanched. "I don't know where you're getting your information."

"From a very reliable source," Nancy said, cutting him off. "I don't have a lot of time to waste. If you won't tell me everything you know about the organization, I'm going to hand over my evidence to the newspaper. And to the police."

Nancy's bluff worked. Andy glanced over his shoulder and lowered his voice to a whisper. "My mother's upstairs. Can we talk outside, please?"

Nancy nodded. She led the way back to the front porch.

Andy closed the door behind them and began to talk. "I'm not really involved with Sea Friends Forever. I mean," he added quickly, "I'm not a member or anything like that. In fact, I think they're kind of crazy. But about a month ago someone called and asked me if I wanted to make some extra money— cash. The job turned out to be working for Sea Friends. They gave us a long list of pranks to pull on the institute. They plan to drive that du Roque guy so crazy that he'll *want* to shut the place down."

"Are other local people being paid by Sea Friends Forever to vandalize the institute?" Nancy asked.

Andy shrugged. "A few. Hey," he added hurriedly, "there was nothing on that list that involved hurting people."

"Do you have any contact with whoever's in charge of this sabotage scheme?"

Andy shook his head. "I know he's from out of town and he organizes this stuff through some local guys he hires."

"That's all?" Nancy said.

"Well, I did hear one of the other guys say the boss was in town, staying on a boat at the marina," Andy went on. "But I haven't heard anything else about him. I don't even know his name."

"Do you know anything about a prank involving one of the aquarium's dolphins?" Nancy asked.

Andy shook his head. "Nope. Nothing on the list about the animals. These guys *love* animals, man. They're, like, obsessed with them."

Nancy believed Andy. At least she believed that if there was a plot to kidnap Whitecap, he knew nothing about it.

"Okay," she said. "Thanks for your help, Andy." She turned and walked down the porch steps. When she got to the bottom she turned. Andy was still standing there. "I'll be in touch."

A little while later Nancy was back at the institute, eating lunch with George, when Ned walked in with Michael Putnam. Ned made his way to Nancy's table as Putnam stopped next to Lynn Harris seated a few tables away. In a voice loud enough for the entire room to hear, Putnam said, "I hope you have good news for me, Lynn."

Lynn shook her head. "No, I'm sorry, Michael, I don't."

"That dolphin had better survive," Putnam said. "Have you figured out yet how he broke free? Was it just an accident or a breach of security? Just how well do you know your team, Lynn? Don't you think that whoever let Whitecap out knew what he was doing?"

"Whitecap's disappearance was no accident," Lynn replied carefully. "But there is absolutely no way any member of my staff is responsible for this."

Lynn stood up and gestured to the others in the room. "Lunch is over, everyone. It's time to start the afternoon search session. Same teams as before, same rules. Meet back here this evening. Be alert. There's a possibility of a storm hitting later. If it heads this way, come in. I don't want anyone to get hurt."

"I'm going to wait for Bess and Jason," George whispered to Nancy and Ned. "We split up this morning to cover more ground."

As others filed out of the room, Dennis got up from his table and walked over to Lynn.

"It's going to be all right," he told her.

"We'll find Whitecap before it's too late. Trust me. I have a good feeling about this."

Lynn forced a smile, and Dennis strode away, but not before casting an angry look at Michael Putnam.

When Dennis was gone, Putnam turned to Lynn again. When he spoke, his voice was cold. "I heard a rumor you might find interesting," he said. "It seems your old friend Matt Folton is the brains—and the money—behind Sea Friends Forever, just as I've always suspected."

Lynn shook her head. "Who told you that? I don't believe it."

Putnam smiled and folded his arms across his chest. "A friend in California, the group's home base. Seems Folton's been supporting the group for some time now, and using his made-for-family-TV animal rights activities as a front for Sea Friends' subversive tactics. Personally," Putnam added, "the whole thing disgusts me."

George shifted beside Nancy. "This is awful," she whispered. "Poor Lynn."

Lynn cleared her throat. "What disgusts me, Michael, is that we're standing here blaming each other for Whitecap's disappearance when we should be working together to bring him home."

Putnam obviously disagreed. Without responding to Lynn, he announced, "If anyone needs me, I'll be in my office working on damage control."

When Putnam had left the room, Nancy walked over to Lynn and put an arm around the older woman's shoulders. She could feel Lynn's body relax, but only for a moment.

Before Nancy could offer a word of support, Jason burst through the cafeteria doors.

He looked as if he'd run miles. His hair was wet and plastered to his head, and mud covered his boots halfway up his shins.

He held up a damp piece of paper. "I found a note—a ransom note. Whitecap's been kidnapped!"

Chapter

Nine

Nancy held Lynn's shoulders tightly as the older woman slumped forward in shock.

"Jason, what does it say?" Ned asked.

Jason looked down at the paper and cleared his throat: " 'It will cost one million dollars for the dolphin's safe return. If you call the police, the dolphin will suffer. More later.' "

Nancy helped Lynn to a seat and then walked over to Jason. She took the letter from his trembling hand and glanced at it.

"Where did you find this, Jason?" she asked.

"When I was coming in for lunch, I remembered there was something wrong with my skiff the last time I used it. I'd forgotten to check it out. I knew we'd be using it on the search this afternoon, and I wanted to make sure it was in good enough condition to take out. I found this note taped to my engine."

Nancy frowned. Jason had found the ransom note. And Jason had been expressing his discontent with the institute ever since Nancy and the others arrived. Was Jason really as disturbed by the kidnapping as he seemed? Or was he somehow involved in it? Nancy turned to Ned. "Maybe we'd better get Mr. du Roque and Michael Putnam over here," she said.

"I'll find them," Ned said, and he left the cafeteria.

"I don't know what we'll do now," Lynn said quietly. "The baby will die within forty-eight hours if he's not reunited with his mother. One million dollars . . ."

"Nancy," George said, "I don't mean to diminish the importance of Whitecap's kidnapping, but I haven't seen Bess in almost two hours. She should have come back for lunch with the rest of us. I'm worried."

"What?" Jason stood. "You mean you haven't seen her since we split up? I'd better go look for her."

Nancy thought about it. At this point, everyone was potentially guilty—or innocent—of the vandalism and of kidnapping Whitecap. But someone had to look for Bess. It might as well be Jason. "Good idea, Jason," she said.

"Why don't you leave the ransom note here. I'll get it to Mr. du Roque and Mr. Putnam."

Jason handed Nancy the note before leaving the room.

"This is outrageous!" Putnam declared. He tossed the ransom note onto a cafeteria table.

"I think we should call the police," du Roque said steadily.

"Didn't you see what the kidnapper said about calling the police?" Putnam demanded. "We'd be signing that dolphin's death warrant."

"For once," Lynn said, "I totally agree with Michael."

Du Roque looked from Putnam to Lynn. "You're not suggesting we pay the million dollars, are you?"

Putnam sighed. "Well, I'm certainly not suggesting we should *not* pay it."

"This might sound like a silly question," George began, "but a million dollars is an awfully large sum of money. What makes the kidnapper think the institute would willingly pay that much for Whitecap's safe return?"

"It's not a silly question, George," Lynn said. "Albino dolphins are rare—"

"And," Putnam interrupted, "Whitecap is to be a major source of revenue for the institute this year, next year, and the year after that. With the right training, he'll become a star attraction. In short, Whitecap's financial value to the institute far exceeds one million dollars. To be blunt, no Whitecap, no institute."

"How about showing some concern for the animal, Michael," Lynn said, "and not just for his dollar value?"

"What do you think, Arman?" Putnam asked. "Don't you agree we should pay the ransom?"

"That will be my decision, Michael," du Roque answered sharply. "It's my institution, and I will make the decision alone."

"Fine," Putnam answered. "But don't forget Sea Friends Forever. If they *are* behind the kidnapping, and the institute doesn't pay for the return of the dolphin, they'll use that fact against us—they'll say we don't care about the animals. If we *do* pay, we'll prove that our ultimate concern is for Whitecap's welfare. And the welfare of all animals. Their protests against us will lose their impact."

"That's a pretty big assumption to make," Nancy began.

"Who asked for your opinion?" Putnam demanded.

"That's enough, Michael," Mr. du Roque

said sternly. "I have asked Ms. Drew to investigate the recent acts of vandalism. She has every right to participate in this discussion."

"I apologize, Ms. Drew," Putnam said. "I didn't know." Putnam looked at his watch. "It's time for me to get back to work." With a brief nod, he left the cafeteria.

"We'll continue this conversation later," du Roque said. "I need a little time to think."

"George, why don't you and I join the search for Whitecap, since Jason is looking for Bess," Ned suggested.

"Good idea," George agreed.

"I'll come with you," Lynn said, leading Ned and George out of the room.

When Nancy and du Roque were alone, du Roque faced her. "Nancy, I'm counting on you to solve this case and to find Whitecap—"

"Yes, Mr. du Roque, I understand," Nancy said.

"Please let me finish," du Roque said, his voice taking on a note of urgency. "I'm counting on you to find the dolphin, Nancy, not because I *won't* pay the kidnappers but because I *can't.* You see, I'm broke."

Nancy walked with du Roque to his office to speak in detail about the institute's financial state.

"Now I understand why the institute has been struggling so hard," Nancy said.

Du Roque nodded. "I meant for the institute to be self-supporting. I shared my estate, I built the facilities, and in the past, I've given large amounts of money to the institute. However, it's the institute's job to generate revenue, through the tourist trade and through gifts and bequests from private benefactors."

"Have private donations fallen off?" Nancy asked.

"Somewhat," du Roque admitted. "But as much as I hate to admit it, the institute's financial trouble rests squarely on my shoulders. I haven't been very smart about letting Michael do the job I hired him to do. The man has a good reputation, and he knows how to raise money, but I've stood in his way, all for the sake of preserving and promoting the academic reputation of the institute. As a result, I might have destoyed my own precious creation."

Nancy frowned. "Is the situation that desperate?"

"Well," du Roque said, with a bitter laugh, "you've seen the result of some of the budget cutbacks. Little security, lots of problems, and I had to let some of the full-time maintenance crew go. Michael has been pushing me to give the institute another infusion of capital, just to help us over this hump. We're having trouble making our payroll and meeting payment deadlines to vendors."

"Can you sell the estate?" Nancy asked.

"I've thought of that," du Roque answered. "But it wouldn't solve the institute's problems. Rocky Isle has no real estate expenses; the land on which it stands is one of my gifts to it. The estate's new owner would undoubtedly demand rent, and an exorbitant one at that."

"Michael and Lynn don't know the truth about your personal financial state, do they?" Nancy said.

"No," du Roque said, "they don't. I've been trying to keep the truth from them, hoping I might come up with a solution to this crisis on my own. Ned has helped to show me how foolish I've been. He's persuaded me to bring in a consultant to help me better understand this kind of enterprise. But you heard Michael a few minutes ago. He thought I would just go ahead and offer one million dollars of my own money as Whitecap's ransom. He and Lynn know the institute doesn't have that kind of money, but they think I do."

Nancy looked directly at du Roque. "If we don't find Whitecap by tomorrow, you're going to have to tell them the truth."

"I know," du Roque answered, closing his eyes as if in pain. "I know."

Nancy walked down a hall of the administration building looking for Michael Putnam's office. When she found it, she knocked on the door. No one answered, so she slowly pushed it open.

She found herself in what appeared to be the reception area where Putnam's assistant, Wendy, sat. The door to the inner office was closed.

Nancy had hoped to talk to Wendy. Well, she would wait a few minutes and see if she returned. In the meantime, she could look around. She closed the door behind her and walked toward Wendy's desk. Sitting on top of the papers in the in-box was a bulky folder labeled "Sea-the-World." Nancy picked it up.

Inside, she found several pieces of correspondence between Michael Putnam and the Sea-the-World directors as well as memos from Lynn and Mr. du Roque and copies of Putnam's memos to them.

Nancy selected a piece of promotional literature first. Sea-the-World was an organization Putnam apparently had sought to associate with Rocky Isle Institute. Nancy quickly ascertained that it was a worldwide chain of marine wildlife tourist attractions.

Nancy then reviewed some of the correspondence between Putnam and Sea-the-World. Putnam's letters to the group suggested that as a Sea-the-World site, Rocky Isle Institute would benefit enormously. And Sea-the-World would gain credibility from Rocky Isle's reputation as a serious research organization.

In a series of memos to du Roque, Lynn, and several major benefactors of the institute, Michael Putnam argued his case eloquently and, Nancy thought, convincingly.

Next, Nancy found a memo from Lynn Harris to Mr. du Roque, arguing against an association with Sea-the-World. Lynn felt that such an association would diminish Rocky Isle's reputation as a top-notch research facility.

Finally, Nancy found a memo from Mr. du Roque, dated only the previous week, rejecting the proposed association. In it, he stated his decision that Rocky Isle Institute should remain an independent entity.

Nancy closed the file and replaced it on top of the in-box. Now she better understood some of Michael Putnam's frustration with Arman du Roque. Why had Mr. du Roque rejected the lucrative association with Sea-the-World when he knew that the institute was in terrible financial trouble?

Nancy understood Lynn's point of view, but Lynn didn't know the extent of the institute's financial difficulties. Clearly, Lynn's coming out against the proposed association with Sea-the-World had seriously strained her working relationship with Michael Putnam.

Nancy's thoughts were interrupted by the sound of high-heeled footsteps approaching the office door. Before she could scoot over to the couch and pretend to be reading a magazine, the door was opened, and Wendy stepped in.

Her hand still on the doorknob, Wendy raised her eyebrows. "May I help you?"

"Hello, Wendy," Nancy said. "It's nice to see you again. We met this morning at the aquarium. I'm Nancy Drew."

"Yes," Wendy interrupted. "I remember. If you're here to see Mr. Putnam, he isn't in."

"I'm here to see you, Wendy, not Mr. Putnam. Mr. du Roque has asked me to investigate the incidents of vandalism at the institute. I thought you might be able to help," Nancy continued.

"How?"

"I understand you and Michael Putnam were involved at one time."

Wendy's face grew red with anger. "What does that have to do with your investigation? It's none of your business."

Nancy walked over to the couch and perched on the edge of it. "Well, actually, Wendy, it is. I need to ascertain the loyalty of the institute's employees. In spite of what might have happened between you and Michael Putnam, you still work for him. That can't be easy."

Nancy paused to watch Wendy's reaction. She looked pained.

"But you also work for Rocky Isle Institute," Nancy continued. "And that's where your loyalty should lie, regardless of what Michael Putnam might have done to you."

Wendy remained silent. Clearly she was not going to defend herself.

After a moment Nancy stood and walked toward the door. "Michael Putnam and Arman du Roque are deeply concerned about Whitecap's disappearance. If he's not found soon, the institute could be in big trouble."

Wendy's harsh laughter surprised Nancy.

"Why in the world would Michael Putnam care whether you find that dolphin or not?" she asked.

"I don't understand," Nancy said.

Wendy leaned on her desk. "Of course you don't," she said. "No matter what he tells you and Arman du Roque, Michael Putnam doesn't care at all about Whitecap's disappearance."

Wendy walked around the desk to stand directly in front of Nancy. "You see," she continued, "Michael Putnam is leaving Rocky Isle at the end of the month. He's accepted the directorship of Sea Kingdom in California. And I'm going with him."

Chapter

Ten

NANCY HAD JUST ENTERED the aquarium's main area to talk to Lynn when Jason staggered in, practically carrying Bess. "Bess!" Nancy cried. "What happened?"

Nancy hurried over to her friend. "Let's get her to a seat." She took Bess's arm and led her to the bleachers.

"I'll get her something hot to drink," Lynn said, hurrying off.

"I found her hobbling back to the institute on one of the paths that lead here from the beach," Jason said.

"What happened?" Nancy asked again.

"It sounds silly, Nan," Bess began. "George, Jason, and I were searching for Whitecap together. At a certain point we separated. I went toward a cliff, not a really high one, to see if I could get a better look at the water. I thought I was far enough back from the edge, but the next thing I knew, I was falling."

She paused and shrugged. "This is going to sound weird, I know. I didn't hear anything or see anyone, but I had the feeling that someone pushed me. I went over the cliff head first." Bess gingerly touched a long, shallow cut on her cheek. "I tumbled all the way down to the beach. I can't believe I didn't get more banged up. I twisted my ankle, but I don't think it's broken. I was stunned, though. I sat there for ages before I stood up and started back here."

Lynn came in and handed Bess a steaming cup of tea.

"Thanks, Lynn," Bess said. "Jason told me about the ransom note. I'm so sorry!"

"So am I," she said. "But I'm glad you're back safe and sound. Well, almost sound."

Bess laughed. "Nothing a little rest and a hot shower won't take care of." She looked at Nancy. "I wish all the problems around here were so easy to fix."

Nancy went out to walk along the path that Bess had been on. While she was trying to figure out what had happened to her friend, she heard someone behind her.

"Nancy!"

Startled, she turned to see Dennis coming up behind her.

"Hi," she called out, hugging herself. "It's getting chilly, isn't it?"

Dennis stopped a few feet from Nancy and laughed. "You don't feel the cold if you've been running after someone."

"Sorry. Have you been following me for long?"

Dennis shook his head. "No. I was just trying to catch up with you so I could give you this." He pulled a folded flyer printed on bright orange paper from the pocket of his slicker. "I found it after lunch, blowing around on the grounds."

Nancy took the flyer from Dennis and read it. It announced a lecture on animal rights to be held the following day at noon at the town hall. The speaker was Matt Folton.

"Why did you think I'd be interested in this?" Nancy asked Dennis.

"Word travels fast around here. I had to drop something off at Putnam's office a little while ago, and Wendy told me you'd been there earlier. She also told me you're looking into the vandalism and Whitecap's disappearance."

Nancy laughed. "Well, I guess everybody will know by dinnertime, huh?"

"Probably." Dennis's expression became

serious. "Nancy, if you ask me, every bad thing that has happened here lately can be blamed on Sea Friends Forever. Look," he said, indicating the flyer Nancy still held. "Matt Folton—Lynn's old friend and, according to Putnam, the brains behind Sea Friends Forever—is in town. What more proof do you need? Sea Friends Forever *has* to be responsible for Whitecap's disappearance."

Nancy bit her lip. She thought of what Andy Gergen had told her about "the boss" being in town recently, living on a boat docked in the marina. Could that be Matt Folton? Could this lecture he was scheduled to give tomorrow be a cover for his illegal activities?

"How did you know about Matt Folton's connection to Sea Friends Forever?" Nancy asked.

"It's no secret around here. Once Putnam got the word from his California friend, he let everyone know. People like Matt Folton are totally destructive to the sort of fund-raising and community-relations-building Putnam does. I don't blame him for telling everyone."

Nancy nodded. "Okay. Thanks, Dennis."

"No problem. See you at dinner." Dennis waved and jogged back the way he'd come.

Nancy watched him until he was out of sight. There was no doubt he was a charmer. But there was also no doubt he was too eager to pin the blame—*all* of the blame—on Sea Friends Forever. Why did it seem so convenient that Dennis had found this flyer on the grounds of the institute? Was he trying to help Nancy? Or was he trying to mislead her? Unfortunately, she had no idea at this point.

A short while later Nancy rang the bell beside the front door of Arman du Roque's mansion. It was five o'clock, and she was hoping that Ned was back from the search and had some free time.

Nancy was shown into the study, where Ned was hard at work.

"Nan!" he said. "What a fantastic surprise!"

Nancy grinned. "If I'd known you'd be so happy to see me, I'd surprise you more often!"

Ned walked over to Nancy and put his arms around her. He bent his head to kiss her gently. When they parted, he sighed. "Why is it, no matter what kind of trip we arrange, we never get to spend time together?"

"Well, today's your lucky day. I was hoping to snag you for the next couple of hours."

"Great," Ned said. "As long as it doesn't have anything to do with an albino dolphin."

"Did anything turn up on Whitecap," Nancy asked.

Ned slowly shook his head.

Nancy plopped down on the big plush sofa,

kicked off her shoes, and curled her legs under her. "I need help checking out Dennis Markwood—and a few other institute employees."

Ned groaned.

Nancy unlocked the large gray file cabinet that contained the institute's employee records.

"You look through Putnam's, Lynn's, and Jason's files, Ned. I'll review Dennis's," Nancy instructed.

"Right." Ned took the folders Nancy held out to him and sat down on one side of the small desk in the file room.

Nancy sat down on the other side, opened Dennis's file and began to read. She hadn't gotten far when she gasped. "Ned, listen to this," she said.

"Has Mr. Charm got a skeleton in his closet?"

"Dennis was head trainer and then assistant director of a place called Sea Universe. From these job descriptions, it sounds a lot like Sea Kingdom, the place where Michael Putnam is supposed to be headed at the end of the month."

"What are you talking about, Nan?" Ned asked.

"Oops, I forgot I hadn't told you yet." She

quickly related the results of her visit with Wendy.

Ned shook his head. "Never a dull moment around here, is there?"

"Nope. But back to Dennis's file. His résumé says he held the position of assistant director at Sea Universe until June of last year. There's a letter from the man who was director at the time—but it's not a letter of recommendation. In fact, it says that Dennis was fired, but it doesn't say why. This is outrageous! I bet Mr. du Roque doesn't know anything about Dennis's trouble at his last job. He told me Putnam did all the hiring."

"Look, Nancy," Ned said, "I don't like the guy, but for all we know, Dennis might have been fired unjustly; it happens all the time. Personality conflicts, you know. Besides, Putnam must have hired him for a reason."

"True," Nancy admitted. "But whatever happened, Dennis went from a job as assistant director of a major recreational facility to one as head tour guide at a small research facility. He's got to be making a lot less money, and the prestige of this job must be negligible compared to that of his old one."

"True," Ned agreed. "But what does any of this prove?"

Nancy sighed and closed Dennis's file. "Nothing. It proves nothing, but it's interesting. Dennis seems to be the most committed member of the senior staff. Maybe he's just grateful to have a job."

"Well," Ned said, "I don't want to disappoint you any more, but Putnam's file and Lynn's *and* Jason's are all as clean as a whistle."

Nancy smiled. "I'm not disappointed. We still have another stop to make before dinner."

"Where are we going now?" Ned asked.

"To the harbormaster's office at the marina," Nancy told him.

As they drove to town, Nancy showed Ned the flyer Dennis had given her earlier.

"Do you see who's speaking at tomorrow's animal rights lecture at town hall? Matt Folton." Nancy reminded Ned of what she'd learned from Andy Gergen about "the boss" being in town and about Michael Putnam's belief that Matt Folton was the brains and money behind Sea Friends Forever.

"Let me guess," Ned said. "You expect to find Matt Folton on a boat docked in the marina."

"I don't expect anything. I just hope."

Nancy swung into a parking space near the harbormaster's office. She and Ned got out of the car and knocked on the door of the small wooden structure.

"Come in!" a voice called.

Nancy opened the door to find a bearded young man sitting behind a desk reading a newspaper.

"Can I help you?"

"I hope so," Nancy said. "We're looking for someone who's docked here at the marina. We don't know his slip number, though." Nancy went on to describe Matt Folton, and before she'd even finished, the harbormaster nodded.

"I know who you mean. He's on *Free At Last,* in the last slip at the end. Can't miss it."

"Thanks a lot," Nancy said as she and Ned hurried out of the office and down the walkway toward Matt Folton's boat.

"There it is." Nancy pointed. No one was on the deck, so they climbed aboard and knocked on the door of the small cabin.

After a few seconds a man pulled the door open halfway and stuck his head out.

It was Matt Folton.

"Mr. Folton," Nancy said smoothly. "I've heard so much about you."

"That's nice," he said, "but I haven't heard a thing about you."

"I'm Nancy Drew, and this is Ned Nickerson. We're both working—volunteering, actually—at the Rocky Isle Marine Institute. Have you heard of it?"

Matt gave a short laugh. "Yes, I've heard of it. What can I do for you?"

"Have you heard about the vandalism and harassment at the institute recently?" Nancy asked.

Matt Folton's face betrayed the slightest smirk. He folded his arms across his chest and said, "Yes, nasty business."

Nancy could feel Ned tense up beside her. "Not as nasty as what happened last night or early this morning, Mr. Folton," Nancy said angrily. "A baby albino dolphin was kidnapped from the institute's aquarium. If he's not found and returned within thirty-six hours, he'll die. Have you heard anything about that, Mr. Folton?"

He looked stunned. "No, I know nothing about the kidnapping. How old is the calf? Are there any leads?"

"That's why we're talking to you," Ned said.

"That's right. We have reason to believe that Sea Friends Forever might be involved in the kidnapping."

Matt Folton didn't comment on the animal rights group. Instead he replied, "I would never, ever harm an animal, any animal. Who could have done such a thing?"

At last Matt came out of the cabin and onto the deck. "Please," he said, "tell me what's going on with Lynn Harris. Is she okay?"

"She's directing the search efforts," Ned said. "She's awfully worried, though."

"Look," Matt said, his tone suddenly urgent, "I need to talk with her. Can you get her to meet me on neutral territory tomorrow morning at nine? There's a café in town called the Coffee Cup. If she doesn't want to come alone, say you'll go with her. We have some unfinished business to settle."

Chapter

Eleven

N<small>ANCY! NED! OVER HERE,</small>" Lynn called, waving them to her table at dinner that night.

Nancy and Ned made their way to Lynn, greeting George, Bess, Evan, Jason, Dennis, Jenny, and Colleen as they progressed. No one looked very cheery.

Nancy sat next to Lynn while Ned went to get them some food.

"How are you?" Nancy asked, concerned by the woman's pale face and the circles under her eyes.

"I've been better," she said. "No luck with the search this afternoon. No one so much as *thought* they saw Whitecap."

Ned returned with their food, and Nancy waited until he was seated before telling Lynn about their conversation with Matt Folton.

"Matt Folton is in town?" Lynn's voice was a whisper, but it couldn't hide her shock. "What's he doing here?"

"He's in town to give a lecture on animal rights in the town hall at noon tomorrow."

"But we think he could be here because he's involved with Sea Friends Forever and maybe the kidnapping," Ned said.

Lynn shook her head. "No way. Matt Folton is passionate in his beliefs, but I can't believe he'd be involved in the kidnapping."

"Well," Nancy went on, "you can ask him yourself. He wants to see you tomorrow at nine o'clock in the morning at the Coffee Cup. He said he wants to help, Lynn."

"What does he want to see me for? I've got enough trouble without adding Matt Folton to the picture. I can't see him tomorrow."

"Why not?" Nancy prodded.

Lynn lowered her eyes. "The day Matt told me I was cruel to train dolphins was the day I knew our friendship was over." Lynn raised her eyes defiantly to Nancy. "I don't want to see him, Nancy."

"Lynn, I know you don't want to hear this," Ned said, "but maybe Matt is involved with Sea Friends. Maybe he's behind the kidnapping. If he is, you might uncover a clue in his conversation. And if he's not involved, he does have a lot of connections and, I'm guessing, a lot of money. He might be able to help fund a rapid emergency search-and-rescue effort."

"Ned's right," Nancy urged. "Come with us. We won't tell Michael about the meeting, and we'll ask Matt to keep it to himself, too."

Nancy and Ned were silent as they waited for Lynn to make her decision. Finally she looked at them and said, "All right. I'll do it, but I want you both there for moral support."

"Nan?"

Nancy turned to see George and Bess standing by the table.

"Hi, guys," Nancy said.

"I'm going to walk back to the cabin with Bess," George said. "She needs a good night's rest, and frankly, so do I."

"Thanks for all your help today," Lynn said. "I'm afraid we're going to need you again tomorrow."

"We'll be ready, Lynn," Bess said.

"Good night, everyone," George called as she and Bess left the cafeteria.

When they were gone, Jason said, "This is making me crazy. I can't stand waiting around to hear from the kidnapper."

"I'm sure we'll hear soon," Nancy said. "We have to be told where to leave the ransom money."

"And then what?" Jason prodded. "Has Mr. du Roque made a decision about whether or not he's going to pay?"

"I hate to say this, Jason, but we can't forget that we're dealing with one or more criminals. We might pay the ransom money and—it's horrible to think about—still never see White-cap again."

"You mean we shouldn't meet the kidnapper's demands?" Jason asked. "I think we should play by his rules and hope for the best."

"I agree with you, Jason," Lynn said. "But I'm not the one holding the purse strings. The decision is Mr. du Roque's."

Nancy looked from Lynn to Jason. If only they knew the truth.

Nancy took Ned's hand as they headed toward the cabins together.

"Let's take the long way back to your cabin," Ned suggested.

"Which way is that?"

Ned shrugged. "I don't know. Just follow me." He pulled her close and wrapped his arms around her waist. Automatically Nancy clasped her hands behind his neck and lifted up her head to kiss him.

"I don't want to get lost, you know," Nancy teased Ned.

"Thanks a lot."

They walked in silence for a few minutes, breathing in the fresh ocean air.

"Penny for your thoughts," Ned said softly.

Nancy sighed. "I can't stop thinking about Whitecap," she said. "It's so sad."

"I know," Ned agreed.

Nancy shook her head. "Oh, Ned, there are so many pieces to this puzzle. I'm afraid we'll never sort it all out in time to save Whitecap."

"Of course we will, Nan," Ned assured her. "Look, we're almost to your cabin. Let's both get some sleep. In the morning maybe we'll have some fresh ideas."

"You're right," Nancy said. "And don't forget, I'm going to Putnam's office early. I'll meet you and Lynn at the Coffee Cup at nine. And, Ned, thanks for walking me home even if it wasn't the long way."

Ned pulled Nancy close for a final goodnight kiss. "You're welcome," he whispered.

As Nancy approached the cabin, she noticed the windows were dark. Good, she thought. Bess and George are getting some rest. Gently, she edged the door open and looked inside. The room was dark, but she could just make out George and Bess's outlines beneath their covers. The only sound was their soft breathing.

Nancy shut the door behind her as gently as she could. She tiptoed over to her own bed and reached for the bedside lamp switch. As soon as she turned it on, there was a loud crackle. Sparks flew everywhere, quickly igniting some papers she'd left on the night table.

Chapter

Twelve

BESS! GEORGE! WAKE UP!" Nancy cried. She darted over to each girl's bed and shook her roughly.

"What? What is it?" Bess mumbled, slowly uncurling from a fetal position.

"Fire!" George yelled, throwing back her covers and leaping from her bed.

"George, grab a blanket and help me smother the flames. The fire's manageable so far. Bess, open the door and the windows."

Nancy studied the lamp socket from which sparks had been pouring a moment ago. Under the lightbulb she found it—a small incendiary device. Just as she suspected, this fire had been set—it was arson. If Nancy hadn't turned the light on and set off the device, it would have sparked while she was sleeping. That could have been deadly.

Training flashlights around the room, Bess and George examined every lamp for more devices. They found none.

Dennis, Evan, and Jason appeared in the open doorway just then.

"What's going on?" Dennis demanded. "We heard you yelling."

"Something was wired into Nancy's lamp to create a fire, but she found it and we put out the flames."

"Is everything all right?" Dennis hurried over to Nancy and grabbed her hands. "Were you hurt, Nancy? Did you inhale any smoke?"

"We're all just fine," Bess said.

"I'll have to call the fire department to make an assessment," Jason said.

"Thanks," Nancy said. "I guess we'll just do without electricity until tomorrow."

"Do you really think the fire was set deliberately?" Dennis asked.

Nancy looked carefully at Jason, Dennis, and Evan. Any one of them could have done it. "Yes, that's exactly what I'm saying."

"It's those crazy Sea Friends!" Dennis said angrily. "I swear, if they hurt anyone on this staff, I'll—"

"Dennis, let's leave it to the fire department," Nancy said. "In the meantime, I'm getting terribly sleepy."

"Right," Jason said, punching in numbers on the phone in the girls' cabin. "If I can get someone to come out now, you can get to sleep very soon."

Dennis and Evan started out the door. "Nancy, if you need anything, just yell," Dennis said.

"Okay," Nancy replied. "Good night—and thanks."

After a quick breakfast and two cups of strong, hot coffee, Nancy made her way to the administration building and Michael Putnam's office. Once again she found the reception area deserted.

She glanced around for something to read. Her eyes wandered to Wendy's in box, where she had found the Sea-the-World file the day before. No files this time. Instead, Nancy spotted a heavy cream-colored envelope with Michael Putnam's name on the front. Nancy reached over and picked it up. She turned it over. Stamped in gold on the flap was the name Folton.

Nancy was about to remove the note from the unsealed envelope when she heard footsteps in the hallway. Almost without thinking, she slipped it into the large outer pocket of her jacket and moved away from the desk.

Nancy could make out a bulky figure through the frosted glass of the door's middle panel. The doorknob turned, and in walked Matt Folton.

"What are you doing here?" Nancy asked abruptly.

Matt, looking startled, replied, "What are *you* doing here?"

"I'm working for Arman du Roque," Nancy said. "I told you that yesterday."

"Well," Matt replied, "I have a reason to be here, too."

"I'm not sure Michael Putnam would agree that you could ever have a good enough reason for being on the institute's property," Nancy replied.

Matt laughed. "Fair enough. I'll tell you exactly why I'm here. I wrote a note to Michael Putnam—a personal note—and I've changed my mind about his reading it. So I came to retrieve it. Unless, of course, he's already read it."

Nancy frowned. "I don't understand. What could you have wanted to say to Mr. Putnam yesterday that you don't want to say this morning?"

Matt didn't have time to answer. Nancy

swung around to face the door just as Michael Putnam walked in.

"Mr. Putnam," Nancy said. "Good morning."

Michael Putnam acknowledged Nancy's greeting with a perfunctory nod and then turned his attention to Matt Folton.

"What are you doing here?" he said coldly.

"I came to see your secretary, Mr. Putnam," Matt replied politely.

"Well," Putnam replied, "she's not here."

Matt acknowledged Putnam's reply with a nod. "I was hoping to take care of my business first thing this morning."

"And what, exactly, is the nature of your business, Mr. Folton?" Putnam asked.

Nancy looked at Matt, who hesitated a moment before speaking.

"I'll call back later when she's in," Matt said, turning to leave.

"Wait a minute, Folton," Putnam called out. "I'm curious about something. What are you doing in Rockport?"

"I'm in town to give a lecture," Matt said. "It's today at noon at the town hall. Come, if you like. You might learn something."

Putnam laughed harshly. "What could I possibly learn from you? How to kidnap a baby dolphin and hold him for ransom? How to destroy the scientific work of a fine institute?"

Nancy held her breath and waited for Matt to explode. But he didn't. Instead, he looked squarely at Putnam and said, "I didn't kidnap Whitecap."

"Get out," Putnam said. "Now!"

Matt nodded to Nancy and, without another word, left the office, closing the door behind him.

"The nerve of him, showing up in my office, trespassing on the institute's property! That man and his band of vandals should be arrested."

"Mr. Putnam," Nancy interrupted, "may I speak to you for a moment?"

Putnam reached into the breast pocket of his blazer and pulled out a folded piece of paper. "We can talk later. Read this."

He handed Nancy the paper. She unfolded it and immediately recognized it as another note from the kidnapper. The typed note was addressed to Michael Putnam, but otherwise it looked the same as the kidnapper's first note.

Nancy read it aloud: " 'Have du Roque leave the million dollars in a black bag at Dogleg Point at 10 tonight. No cops, no company—or the dolphin dies by morning. If the money shows up, you receive instructions at 10:45 on where to find the dolphin.'"

"We have to let du Roque know about this right away," Putnam said, slipping the note back into his pocket. "I just stopped by to pick up some papers. If you'll wait a moment, we can go up to the mansion together."

Du Roque shook his head and handed the note back to Putnam. "I cannot believe we have less than twenty-four hours in which to find Whitecap. The last thing I want to do is give in to a kidnapper's demands! I think it's time we called in the police."

"No, Arman!" Putnam said loudly. "That's the last thing we should consider right now. That dolphin's life is too important. We have to believe the kidnapper is serious when he says he'll kill Whitecap if we call the police."

Du Roque questioned Nancy, "What do you think?"

"I agree with Mr. Putnam. For the moment, I think we should continue our search efforts, step them up, if possible."

"Yes, yes," du Roque said, rubbing his hands together. "I'll talk to Lynn immediately. Maybe helicopters . . ."

Putnam shook his head. "Arman, I'll speak

with Lynn and we'll see what we can do, within the budget, of course. Let's meet this evening in my office at seven and make a final decision. In the meantime, Arman, you work on getting the ransom money together."

Chapter

Thirteen

NANCY ARRIVED in town early for her 9:00 A.M. meeting with Lynn, Matt, and Ned. She sat down on a bench in the village green and pulled out Matt Folton's letter to Michael Putnam. The note was written with diplomacy and sincerity. Matt Folton was offering to make peace with Rocky Isle Institute as well as with Michael Putnam and Arman du Roque, personally.

"When I heard about the kidnapping of your institute's albino dolphin calf," he had written, "I finally realized that the life of one creature is much more valuable than any number of lofty ideas."

"I'll take that, please."

Nancy whirled to face Matt Folton, who had

come up behind her. Before she could stop him, he grabbed the note from her hand.

"I don't understand," Nancy said. "Why didn't you want Mr. Putnam to read that note?"

"After I spoke to you and Ned yesterday," he said slowly, coming around the bench, "I did some serious thinking. I realized it was time to reconsider my approach to the animal rights movement. As a first gesture, I wrote this note to Michael Putnam and asked a kid who works at the dock to deliver it. But by this morning I'd changed my mind."

"Why?" Nancy insisted.

"Because Lynn Harris won't return my calls. In fact, the guy who answered the phone was downright rude and made it clear that he doubted Lynn would want to speak to me. Then I found out that Michael Putnam had rented a cabin cruiser for tonight. He's got a kidnapped dolphin calf to worry about and he's renting a pleasure craft? That made me think maybe the people at Rocky Isle don't really care after all."

"Oh, Matt," Nancy replied, "don't jump to conclusions. Come with me to the Coffee Cup and talk to Lynn yourself. Maybe she never got your messages. I do know she's planning to meet us this morning."

Matt shrugged. "Okay, I'll talk to her. But how do you explain Putnam's behavior in the middle of a crisis?"

"I can't," Nancy admitted. "Come on, let's find Ned and Lynn."

Nancy and Matt entered the Coffee Cup and slipped into the booth where Lynn and Ned were already seated.

"It's been such a long time, Lynn," Matt said. "You look good."

"Thanks, you look good, too." She smiled tentatively. "A bit more weather-worn maybe . . ."

Matt laughed. "Years of working outdoors can do that to you. Visiting sites, leading protests."

Now that he'd introduced the topic they were here to discuss, Nancy was not about to let it go. "Lynn," she said, "I told Matt about Whitecap's kidnapping."

Lynn looked hard at Matt, as if she could determine the truth of his statement by reading his face. "Matt," she said, "I have to know. Are you involved with Sea Friends Forever?"

Matt glanced briefly at Nancy, who sat diagonally across from him. Then he looked back at Lynn and nodded.

Lynn slammed her hands on the table. "Do

you know how much trouble you and your group has caused us? We can barely get our work done, we're so busy cleaning up after one attack and trying to prevent the next one."

Matt smiled ruefully. "That was the point, Lynn," he admitted. "Our goal was to interrupt your work so that you would shift your attention from *what* you were doing to *defending* what you were doing. The point was to make you all *think*. Textbook activism," he added weakly.

"Well, you failed the course," Lynn replied. "I promise you, if that dolphin calf dies because of you and your . . . your . . ."

"Hold on, Lynn," Matt said forcefully. "I had nothing to do with the kidnapping. Sea Friends Forever had nothing to do with it. That's not the sort of thing we would do. Ever."

"What *is* the sort of thing you and Sea Friends would do?" Nancy asked quietly. "Tell us, Matt. Would you send people dressed as dolphins to crash an invitation-only event and throw fish blood and guts at Michael Putnam? Or fire a smoke bomb at a group of defenseless people on a small boat in the middle of the ocean?"

Matt sighed and ran a hand through his hair. "Yes, those are things we would do."

"And it was you I met that night on the grounds, wasn't it?" Nancy asked.

Matt looked sheepish now. "You have some kick, Nancy."

"What were you doing on the grounds at night?" Ned asked.

"I was scouting for Sea Friends," he explained. "We were planning to mess up some of the major walking paths just before the institute opens for the season. I didn't expect to meet anyone. I think I was more scared than you, Nancy."

"Was messing up the paths also meant to distract us, Matt?" Lynn asked angrily. "I'm sorry, but I find your tactics ill-conceived and cowardly."

Matt frowned. "Wasn't it cowardly of you not to accept my calls, Lynn?"

"What? I don't know what you're talking about," Lynn said. "When did you call?"

"Yesterday afternoon. I left four messages."

"Well, I never got them. You probably spoke to Dennis Markwood, our head tour guide. He has absolutely no tolerance for Sea Friends Forever or for anyone associated with the group."

"Before we get off the subject," Ned broke in, "were you responsible for the rock thrown through a window in Nancy's cabin? And the warning note that accompanied it?"

Matt looked genuinely puzzled. "Now you have me at a disadvantage. I don't know anything about a broken window or warning note."

Nancy nodded. "What about Bess? Someone pushed her down a small cliff on the institute's grounds."

Matt shook his head. "No, I know nothing about that, either. Of course, there's always a chance that a member of Sea Friends acted without my knowledge or permission. I'll find out if any of my people were responsible."

"One more thing," Nancy said. "Were you responsible for setting the electrical fire in my cabin last night?"

"What!" Ned grabbed Nancy's hands across the table. "Why didn't you tell me?"

"Ned, it's all right. No one was hurt. I threw a blanket over the flames, and the fire department came to check it out. An electrician is coming this morning to fix the lamp. George and Bess are waiting for him to show up this morning."

"Listen to me," Matt said urgently. "I had no knowledge of the fire, either. I swear. Lynn," he went on, "I've been doing a lot of thinking lately. A lot of thinking about what happened to us, our friendship, and what I've been doing with my life. I know that you have every reason to hate me. But will you let me help you find Whitecap?"

After what seemed like a long time, Lynn spoke. "I've missed you, Matt," she said softly. "And I accept your help."

Nancy made plans to meet Matt at the marina later that afternoon, and she told Ned and Lynn about the evening meeting in Putnam's office. Then Nancy and Ned climbed into the Mustang and headed for the boardinghouse where Putnam lived.

"Why do you want to go there now? Isn't Putnam in his office?" Ned asked.

"Exactly. I need to get a look at Mr. Putnam's room."

"Why? What are you looking for?" Ned asked as he made a left turn onto Maple Street.

"I'm not sure. Something Matt told me this morning suddenly clicked. It's a long shot, but I have to take the chance. Pull in beyond the house," Nancy directed as they approached number 35.

Ned parked the Mustang and looked at Nancy. "I suppose I don't need to tell you to be careful," he said.

"You don't. But it's nice that you do." Nancy kissed Ned and got out of the car.

After a quick glance up and down the block, Nancy walked up the drive and opened the unlocked door. Once inside, she was greeted by a friendly woman in her late fifties.

"May I help you?" the woman asked.

"Hi. My name is Nancy Drew. I work for Michael Putnam at the Rocky Isle Marine Institute. He forgot an important file, and he sent me to get it. He said it's in his room."

"No problem," the woman responded. "His room is the last door on the right."

"Thanks a lot," Nancy said. "I'd better hurry before he starts wondering why I've been gone so long."

Nancy dashed up the staircase and hurried to the last door on the right. She went inside, then closed and locked the door behind her.

The room was well kept and homey. The bed had already been made and the wastebasket emptied.

She decided to start with the desk. One by one, Nancy opened the drawers. Nothing. Not even a stray scrap of paper. Next she examined each drawer of the bureau. Nothing but neatly folded clothes. Next she checked the closet. Nothing unusual there. She slid a large suitcase down from the top shelf of the closet and laid it on the bed. It was unlocked. And it was empty.

Frustrated, Nancy put everything back exactly where she'd found it. Hands on her hips, she looked around the room again. She noticed a sport coat hanging on the back of a chair and decided to check the pockets. She pulled a piece of paper out of one of them. It was a receipt for the rental of a cabin cruiser, to be picked up at nine o'clock that night. The receipt was marked "Paid in full."

"This is it," Nancy whispered. She returned the receipt to the pocket and draped the sport coat over the chair once more. The rental agency, Charlie's Charters, was sure to have a copy of the receipt. She didn't want Putnam to return to the room before his getaway that evening and realize the receipt was missing. He'd know someone was onto him and would immediately make a run for it. Then the institute would never recover Whitecap.

Nancy was walking to the door when the phone rang. She jumped at the sound. Where was it? Then she saw it, a small phone and answering machine combination, on the bureau. She stood and waited for the ringing to stop. When it did, Michael Putnam's voice filled the room.

Nancy waited for the beep, her heart racing. Who was calling Putnam at home during a workday? A man. A voice that was familiar, but one that she couldn't immediately place.

"The dolphin is fine right now. But if anything goes wrong tonight, he'll be in trouble. He won't last forever out there, Putnam, and don't forget, we agreed to return him. Then you'll resign and head out to Sea Kingdom. A week or two later you call me with the offer we discussed. Nothing could be simpler. Don't blow it."

Then the voice laughed and Nancy knew who it was.

Dennis.

Chapter

Fourteen

I SHOULD HAVE KNOWN," Nancy murmured. She dashed over to the bureau and then stopped short. The integrated phone and answering machine contained a microchip, not a tape. Taking the tape for evidence was not an option.

Nancy hurried down the stairs and out the front door of the boardinghouse. A few seconds later she slid into the Mustang beside Ned. "You're not going to believe what I just found," she began. As they drove off, Nancy told Ned about the charter receipt and the message from Dennis.

"So that's why Dennis didn't tell Lynn about Matt's calls," Ned mused. "He was trying to prevent a reconciliation before the big payoff tonight. He knew that if we could eliminate Matt and Sea Friends Forever as suspects, we'd have to look elsewhere. And maybe we'd find out that Dennis was responsible for the kidnapping."

"Right," Nancy agreed. "And if Putnam is the brains behind the scheme, Dennis is the muscle. It makes sense. Dennis has experience with the animals, something that Putnam doesn't have. Putnam needed Dennis to pull off the kidnapping, and Dennis needed Putnam to put his career back on track."

"And now," Ned added, "Putnam is planning to back out of their deal by running off with the million dollars. In addition to the job of assistant director at Sea Kingdom, Dennis was probably going to get a cut of whatever money Putnam could choke out of Mr. du Roque."

"No matter how angry Dennis will be when he discovers that Putnam reneged, he won't be able to say anything," Nancy said, "without implicating himself in the process."

Ned stopped at a traffic light. "The one who's going to get the biggest surprise is Putnam, when he discovers that Mr. du Roque doesn't have one million dollars to give away."

Nancy frowned as they drove on again. "We have to play this very carefully."

"I don't think we have much of a choice," Ned said. "The chances are good we won't find Whitecap before tonight. Dennis has probably made sure of that. I think we have to play along, have Mr. du Roque make the drop-off, and then catch Putnam red-handed."

Nancy nodded. "And we still can't call in the police," she said. "We can't risk spooking Putnam or Dennis. We'd never see Whitecap again." Nancy paused. Finally she said, "I think we should go to Mr. du Roque, tell him we think we know who the kidnapper is, and tell him it's best if you and I keep the name to ourselves until the very end. He won't like it, but maybe he'll agree."

"Good idea," Ned agreed. "Mr. du Roque might jump the gun and accuse Putnam before we can definitely pin anything on him. And if we're keeping Mr. du Roque in the dark, maybe we shouldn't tell Lynn or Jason, either."

They pulled into the institute grounds, and Ned parked outside the aquarium. "There is someone we should tell, though," Nancy said as they got out of the car.

"Who?" Ned asked.

"Matt Folton. If we're going to catch Michael Putnam in the act, we need Folton, and we need his boat."

"You were right, Nancy," George said. "It was arson. The cabin could have burned down."

Nancy and Ned had met George and Bess by Chelsea's tank. As they watched Whitecap's mother circle, Nancy told her friends what she had learned from Matt Folton and from poking around Michael Putnam's room.

"I always thought that Dennis was a little too charming to be real," Bess said dryly.

"And I always thought he was a little too flirty for his own good," Ned added slyly.

Nancy smiled. "I don't flatter myself by believing that Dennis liked me," she said. "I think he was just trying to throw me off his trail by pretending to like me."

"Hey, Ned, you should be happy that Nancy didn't fall for him," George teased.

Nancy grinned. "Well, he does look pretty good in a tux."

"Mr. du Roque?" Nancy said a little while later. She stood just inside his office, the door half open behind her. "May I come in?"

Du Roque, sitting at his desk, looked up from his work. "Oh, Nancy, of course, sit down." She took a seat across from him.

"Have you brought me good news about Whitecap?" Mr. du Roque asked.

"No, not yet. I think I know who the kidnappers are, though."

"Nancy! That's wonderful! Who? Have you called the police?"

"That's what I want to talk to you about. Ned and I have discussed this, and we both feel that we should proceed this evening without revealing what we know to anyone."

Du Roque shook his head. "You mean you won't even tell me?"

Nancy leaned forward and spoke earnestly. "Mr. du Roque, you've placed your trust in me so far, and for that I'm very grateful. I have to ask that you continue to trust me for another few hours. Please."

Du Roque was silent for a moment. Finally he replied, "Okay, we'll do it your way."

Nancy let out a sigh of relief. "Here's what I need you to do. We'll meet at Mr. Putnam's office at seven o'clock tonight. You'll be carrying a bag containing what everyone will think is one million dollars in cash. In fact, it will contain only a few thousand dollars, which I'm sure you'll come up with." Du Roque quickly nodded. "Underneath those bills, filling about two-thirds of the bag, will be stacks of plain paper, cut in the shape of bills. I'm counting on the kidnappers' not taking the time to examine all the stacks of bills. I'll be back to help you in a little while."

Nancy made a quick call to her father and ate some lunch before taking off for the marina to meet Matt.

"I can't believe it," Matt said. He and Nancy were seated in the cramped cabin of his boat at a little after three o'clock. "Michael Putnam is the kidnapper? But why would he throw away a successful career?"

Nancy shrugged. "One million dollars is a nice sum with which to start a new life. Anyway, we need to look at a map to figure out where to catch him."

Matt spread out a map of the entire coastal area surrounding Rocky Isle and drew a large circle around Dogleg Point, where du Roque was to leave the money.

"I'll meet you and Ned here," Matt said, drawing another, smaller circle around a small cove on one side of the point. "Putnam will have to approach the point from this direction," he explained, drawing a line from the town marina to Dogleg Point. "He won't see us as he pulls in to retrieve the money. When he pulls out again, we'll follow him from where we're hidden."

"How are we going to stop him, though, Matt?"

"Nancy, I've spent a lot of my life on boats. Trust me, we'll get him. No matter what it takes."

Chapter

Fifteen

"Where do we go from here, Michael?" Lynn asked, when everyone was gathered in Putnam's office.

"We make sure we all know exactly what to do this evening," Putnam said. "Arman, do you have the money?"

Du Roque lifted the black leather bag that sat at his feet. "Yes, Michael, one million dollars. In cash."

"Good. You'll deliver the bag to Dogleg Point at exactly ten o'clock."

Jason interrupted, "I know the kidnapper wanted Mr. du Roque to be alone, but it's too dangerous. I think I should go with him."

"That's a good idea," Nancy said. "Mr. Putnam, what do you think?"

"Well," Putnam responded, as if giving the

notion serious thought, "I suppose the kidnapper can't object to someone's being with Arman, as long as they both leave after Arman drops the money. Yes, that sounds okay."

"Very well," du Roque answered.

"Now," Putnam continued, "I'll stay here in my office and wait for word from the kidnapper. I'm assuming he'll contact me, since he addressed his last note to my attention. When I get his call, I'll relay the information about Whitecap's whereabouts to Lynn and her team, who will be waiting at the dock, ready to make the recovery. Is that clear, Lynn?"

Lynn nodded. "Perfectly," she said. "You call my cell phone so we can head out immediately. Jason, once you've accompanied Mr. du Roque back to the institute, you'll join us."

"Absolutely," Jason agreed.

Putnam stood and clasped his hands in front of him. "Well, are we all set? If so, and if all goes well, we'll meet back here after Whitecap has been successfully reunited with his mother."

Nancy and Ned were back at Nancy's cabin, getting ready to meet Matt at the cove. Before they left, Nancy received a phone call from her dad.

"What's up?" Ned asked after Nancy had hung up.

"I called Dad earlier today and asked him if he could find out about Dennis's background. You know, see if Dennis had been arrested, if he had a criminal record, or anything else unusual. Dad just called to tell me what he'd found óut. Look at this," Nancy said, handing Ned the piece of paper she had taken notes on.

Ned whistled. "Wow, Dennis was fired because he embezzled money from Sea Universe?"

"And there were rumors he tried to sell a few of the animals to an organization claiming to be a research lab," Nancy said grimly. "Can you believe it?"

"No wonder Putnam hooked up with him," Ned commented. "Come on. Let's go meet Matt."

"What a snake. The more I think about him, the angrier I get. Wishing us luck—what incredible nerve!"

"He won't be so calm and collected in a little while," Ned reminded her.

"I know," Nancy agreed.

They hid Nancy's car at the marina and made their way toward the cove on foot. "Look, there's Matt," Nancy whispered.

"Hey," Matt called. "Come on."

When Nancy and Ned had joined Matt on the boat, Nancy checked her watch. "Okay, guys, now we keep an eye out for du Roque and Jason to make the drop, and then we wait for Putnam to come along for the pickup."

Ned stationed himself on the port side of the boat and, binoculars in place, peered at Dogleg Point. Nancy took her binoculars from their case and stationed herself in the bow. Matt was in charge of the boat. Now all they could do was wait.

At exactly ten o'clock, Nancy, peering through her binoculars, saw Arman du Roque and Jason Kalb pick their way around the large rock at Dogleg Point. She saw du Roque place the bag filled with money and blank paper on a small ledge behind the rock, turn, and make his way back. In a minute, he and Jason were out of sight again.

"They did it," Nancy whispered, drawing her jacket around her to keep out the chill night air. The wind had suddenly picked up, making the night unpleasantly cold.

"This is it," Matt said.

No more than ten minutes later, through the whistle of the rising wind, Nancy heard the low thrum of an engine. It had to be Michael Putnam's boat. When the sound of the engine died away, she assumed that Putnam had anchored on the far side of the point. A few minutes later she saw a figure wearing bulky all-weather clothing climb around the rock: Putnam. When he spotted the bag on the ledge, he picked it up and began the awkward climb back around the rock to his boat.

"Here we go," Ned said.

Matt stood ready at the wheel. They waited and watched as Putnam pulled away from Dogleg Point. When he was a little way out from shore, he suddenly accelerated.

"Hold on!" Matt cried. He started the engine and steered the boat away from the coast.

"Can we catch him?" Ned cried.

"We have to try," Matt answered. "He's got a cabin cruiser. It can't go as fast as we can. Putnam didn't count on a high-speed chase."

Just then Nancy heard Putnam accelerate again. "He knows he's being followed," she shouted back to Matt. She put the binoculars to her eyes and saw Putnam glance over his shoulder. Yes, he knew.

Matt leaned on the throttle and the boat picked up speed, its front end rising slightly above the surface of the water. Cold ocean spray hit Nancy's face like a handful of needles. She squinted and ducked her head to wipe her eyes clear of the stinging water. Then she gripped the gunwale of the boat with her free hand and raised the binoculars once again. Through the salt-spattered lenses she watched Putnam hunch over the wheel, as if urging his craft to go faster. But Matt was gaining on him. When they caught up to

Putnam, Nancy knew she'd have to act quickly. They needed to secure Putnam—and they also needed him to reveal Whitecap's whereabouts.

"Hold on!" Matt shouted. Nancy gripped the gunwale with both hands as Matt pushed the engine to its limit. A moment later the *Free At Last* pulled up alongside Putnam's rented cabin cruiser. Putnam glanced over at Nancy, then slowed down and cut the engine. Matt also slowed and cut his engine.

From his rocking boat, Putnam shouted, "Nice work, Ms. Drew. I'm impressed."

Nancy shouted back. "Where's Whitecap?"

Putnam laughed. Carried on the cold wind, his voice had the sting of malice. "You're crazy if you think I'm going to tell you that now! I won't radio Lynn until the three of you are back on land. Do you understand me?"

"Why should we even believe Whitecap is still alive?" Matt called out.

"You're just going to have to take my word for it, aren't you? You've been very foolish, all of you. It's ten forty-five exactly—the time I was scheduled to contact Lynn Harris. If you hadn't followed me, the rescue team would be on its way to retrieve Whitecap right now."

Nancy stole a glance at her watch. Putnam was right. Lynn would be waiting for the call.

"What makes you think that if we let you go you won't get caught?" Matt called out.

"Because if there's one thing I'm sure of it's that you people are desperate to get that dolphin back. You'd do anything, even let me escape."

"Look, Putnam—" Ned began.

"No, *you* look!" Putnam's voice was full of rage. "I've had enough of penny-pinching, fantasy-minded millionaires, psychopathic protesters, and animal-loving scientists. Sea Kingdom would have been more of the same, wrapped in a glossier package. I'm off to make a comfortable new life for myself. Now," he added, regaining a measure of control, "pull out your radio and toss it to me."

Nancy turned to Ned. "Go ahead, Ned," she instructed. "Do as he says." Ned slid the radio out of its mount and threw it over to Putnam's boat. It clattered onto the deck.

"All right, now start your engine, Folton," Putnam called.

"Nancy, I . . ." Matt began.

"Do it, Matt," Nancy replied, her eyes on Putnam as she crept slowly toward the rail, her movements disguised by the rise and fall of the boat on the ocean swells.

As Matt turned the key in the ignition, and as Putnam grinned, Nancy stepped up onto the gunwale and hurled herself through the air. With a loud thud, she landed on the deck of Putnam's boat. As she scrambled to her feet, she heard Ned shout her name and Matt cut the engine of the *Free At Last*.

Putnam uttered a cry of rage and lunged for Nancy. The deck was too slippery for her to gain her balance before he grabbed her, swung her around, and twisted her left arm behind her back. He threw his right arm around her chest and grasped her left shoulder.

"You'll never get away with this, Putnam," Nancy gasped through her pain. She could feel him nudging her closer to the rail. She planted her bent legs as firmly as she could against the deck and resisted his pushing.

Using all of her strength, Nancy elbowed Putnam in the gut with her free arm. With a grunt, he relaxed his hold on her just long enough for Nancy to lunge forward and break away. She slammed into the rail and steadied herself against it. Then she whirled around to face Putnam.

He made another run for her. Nancy quickly assumed a fighting stance and, when Putnam was close enough, aimed a flying kick at his head.

Putnam fell flat on his back. Before he could recover his senses, Nancy dropped on top of him and pinned his shoulders to the deck with her knees.

Then she heard Ned land on the deck behind her. "Ned, get the mike!"

Ned scampered over to where Putnam lay and thrust the radio mike at Nancy. "Move over, Nan, I've got him," he instructed.

Nancy let Ned take her place. She knelt beside Putnam and put the mike up to his face.

"Make the call," she demanded hoarsely.

Chapter

Sixteen

AT ABOUT NINE O'CLOCK the following morning, Nancy and her three friends stood by the side of the tank, watching Chelsea play with her baby. Whitecap leaped into the air, and Nancy ducked to avoid the splash his body made when he dived back into the water.

"Did Dennis put up a fight last night?" Ned asked.

"Do you mean when the police arrested him," George asked, "or earlier in the evening, when Bess bored him half to death with stories of her fifty favorite outfits?"

"I did not bore him," Bess protested. "I was just trying to keep him from falling asleep listening to your stories of all the tennis games you won last summer. I mean, really, George, how self-centered can you get?"

Bess then grinned and said, "George *was* pretty spectacular. When Dennis saw the police cars pulling up to the museum building, he tried to make a run for it. George ran after him, dived for his legs, and tackled him to the ground. It was so cool!"

"Cool, yeah, but I've got terrible scrapes on my knees," George said ruefully.

"You're lucky you don't have burns." Nancy turned to see Jason walking toward them.

"The police are with du Roque in his office," Jason said. "I just came from there."

"And?" Bess prompted.

"And they found Dennis's fingerprints in the cabin. The police questioned him, and he admitted to rigging the fire."

"Why?" George asked. "Just to scare us off?"

Jason shrugged. "I guess. The same reason he pushed Bess off that cliff," he added. "He confessed to that, too."

"I knew I wasn't imagining things," Bess said. "That creep."

"You know," Nancy said, "it's really too bad about Dennis. He was building a good career, he'd achieved a position as assistant director of a major marine entertainment park, and then something made him go wrong."

Ned said, "Or maybe Dennis made something go wrong."

"Maybe." Nancy shrugged. "Maybe his greed got the better of him. Embezzling funds, trying to sell the very animals he was bound to protect. Dennis has a lot of problems."

"All that charm down the drain." George sighed. "Well, you know what they say about charm without substance."

That night at dinner the mood was lively. For the first time in days, laughter rang out around the room. Arman du Roque had asked Lynn to replace Michael Putnam, and she had gladly accepted. Even Wendy was going to stay on. Nancy smiled when she saw the two women eating dinner together.

Ned passed Nancy a plate of rolls, and she took one before passing it to Jenny. She and Colleen had just learned of the kidnapping and of Dennis's and Putnam's guilt.

"I still can't believe Dennis is guilty!" Colleen wailed.

"Nancy, did you suspect him from the beginning?" Jenny asked, her face serious. "I mean, did you know just by looking at him that he was one of the bad guys?"

"Yeah, like were you able to tell from his eyes or something?" Colleen stuffed half a buttered roll in her mouth.

Nancy took advantage of the momentary silence. "No, no, and no," she said. "You can rarely tell the truth about people just by looking at them. Most of us hide a lot of ourselves. Some of us are better at deception than others, that's all."

Jenny frowned in concentration. "I think I understand." Then she sighed. "It's too bad, though. Dennis was really cute."

"Uh, so, are you girls going to stick around for the rest of the preseason?" Nancy asked quickly.

Jenny brightened. "Oh, yeah. We're having a good time, even without Dennis. I mean, the work is hard, but it's for a good cause. And Whitecap is so cute!"

Colleen nodded. "We're going to tell our friends to come next year. The experience is definitely worth the hard work. Living away from your parents, even if they're only a couple miles away, is cool!"

Nancy thought of her father and of how he'd come through for her. "Oh, very cool, I guess," she said with a smile.

Nancy and Ned leaned against the rail of Chelsea and Whitecap's tank the next afternoon. They were quiet, and, even better, they were alone.

"It'll be hard to say goodbye to the dolphins," Nancy said softly.

"Yeah, it will," Ned agreed. "It'll be hard to say goodbye to everyone here."

"Did you hear about Matt?" Nancy asked.

Ned straightened. "No. What?"

"Lynn told me. He's resigning from Sea Friends Forever. No more financial support, no more leadership role. He told Lynn he's done some serious soul-searching and he's decided to make a big contribution to the institute."

"That's fantastic," Ned said, drawing Nancy into his arms. "Well, I'm ready to get back to reality and hit the books in a few days. How about you?"

"Definitely," Nancy replied, a twinkle in her eye. "The real world sounds easy after all the mystery and hard work in the animal world."

Nancy's next case:

Nancy's in San Francisco, and the city's a real knockout . . . in more ways than one. She sees a woman being hit over the head in the famed Presidio, but Nancy is unable to nab the assailant and she can't identify the victim—who's been struck with amnesia. The victim's sketchbook is the only clue to the crime, and as Nancy puts the pieces together, a sinister picture begins to emerge. The woman is Lilly Lendahl, a budding artist and potential heiress trapped in a tangled web of deception, jealousy, and greed. And hidden in the web is someone with a very long memory for murder . . . in *Strange Memories,* Case #122 in The Nancy Drew Files™.

THE HARDY BOYS CASEFILES

**Do your younger brothers and sisters
want to read books like yours?**

**Let them know there
are books just for *them!***

They can join Nancy Drew and her best
friends as they collect clues and solve
mysteries in

THE NANCYDREW NOTEBOOKS®

Starting with
#1 The Slumber Party Secret
#2 The Lost Locket

AND

**Meet up with suspense and mystery
in Frank and Joe Hardy:
The Clues Brothers™**

#1 The Gross Ghost Mystery
#2 The Karate Clue

Look for a brand-new story every
other month at your local bookseller

A MINSTREL® BOOK

Published by Pocket Books

1359